AT THE
CROSSROADS

Also by Travis Hunter

Two the Hard Way

AT THE CROSSROADS

TRAVIS HUNTER

KENSINGTON PUBLISHING CORP.

www.kensingtonbooks.com

DAFINA BOOKS are published by

Kensington Publishing Corp.
119 West 40th Street
New York, NY 10018

All Kensington titles, imprints, and distributed lines are available at special quantity discounts for bulk purchases for sales promotion, premiums, fund-raising, educational, or institutional use.

Special book excerpts or customized printings can also be created to fit specific needs. For details, write or phone the office of the Kensington Special Sales Manager: Kensington Publishing Corp., 119 West 40th Street, New York, NY 10018. Attn. Special Sales Department. Phone: 1-800-221-2647.

Dafina and the Dafina logo Reg. U.S. Pat. & TM Off.

ISBN-13: 978-0-7582-4251-8
ISBN-10: 0-7582-4251-4

First Printing: December 2010
10 9 8 7 6 5 4 3 2 1

Printed in the United States of America

This book is dedicated to the memory of my father, Louis N. Johnson.

Acknowledgments

I would like to thank God for His many blessings. Rashaad Hunter, my son, who never ceases to amaze me: You're the best kid a dad could ask for. Linda Hunter, my mother, for all that you've done and continue to do. Carolyn Rogers, PhD; Sharon Capers; Andrea Gilmore; Avery, LaShay, and Travon Moses; James Moses; Ron Gregg; Ayinde, Ahmed, Jibade, and Tailor Johnson; Mary and Willard Jones; and Tee C. Royal for the early reads and the kind words. Sara Camilli, Selena James, Adeola Saul, and all of the hardworking people at Kensington Publishing Corporation. And to the wonderful people of The Hearts of Men Foundation—we are doing very good work in the communities we serve and are changing young lives for the better.

1

Franklin "Franky" Bourgeois lay flat on his back staring at a ceiling that had long lost its shine. The white paint was old and water stained. The ceiling fan was missing two blades and made a *whopping* sound as it went around and around. He was sweating like a pig in a slaughterhouse. Atlanta had been experiencing a terrible heat wave for the last few days, and he was feeling its effects. There was no air conditioner in the house, and only an occasional breeze came from the open window or the broken fan above his head.

He heard his cousins' voices out in the living room of the small, dilapidated ranch-style house they called home. As usual, they were arguing about something. He was tired of them and tired of living the ghetto life that he had been so enamored with just a few years ago. Now he wondered why God was playing such a cruel joke on him. He wanted to go back to the way things were before nature turned his city into a giant swimming pool. When Hurricane Katrina came through New Orleans, she turned his entire life upside down. He went from being a straight A student with a loving dad to an orphan with two derelicts for cousins. Passed away from cancer, a year before the hurricane, and although losing her had been hard, Katrina was worse. He had always been a daddy's boy. His mother had been sweet, but she had spent most of her time working. His dad had worked out of their home, so they had become very close.

Franky couldn't shake the feeling that his life was just a bad dream, and he kept thinking that one day he would wake up and see his mother cooking breakfast as she rushed around their five-bedroom house in the Garden District. He closed his eyes and visualized her barking orders as she rushed him to get ready for school. He had hated it then, but he would give his right arm to hear her yell at him now. He'd have given the other arm to have his father jack him for complaining under his breath about doing his petty chores.

For the last three years, Franky had been severely depressed. The only inkling of peace came when he was unconscious, which explained why he slept twelve hours out of every day. When he was asleep, he was free. He didn't have to worry about food, violence, homelessness, or any of the other troubles that accompanied his conscious state. But the most important reason he slept all day was because in his dreams, there was a good chance he could be with his parents. His dreams were always so vivid and real, and when he woke up and realized that it was all in his mind, he was usually angry and sad for the rest of the day. He missed them so much.

Franky pulled his tall, lanky body up from the well-used

mattress and looked at his watch. It was two forty-five in the afternoon, and he had slept yet another day away. He heard the rumbling of a school bus outside his window, followed by the joyful sounds of the elementary-school kids laughing and playing. He walked over to the window and looked out at the ghetto that was now his home. The kids always made him happier. Their innocence and joyfulness gave him hope that all was not bad in the world. He smiled and realized that he hadn't smiled in a long time. His innocence had been taken away when he lost the life he once had. He was fifteen years old, yet he felt like a fifty-five-year-old man.

"Jason," he called out to the little boy who lived across the street from him. "Bring your lil nappy-headed self over here."

Jason was seven years old and was always in some type of trouble. His teachers were completely fed up with him, and his grandmother, Mrs. Bertha, was almost to the point of strangling him to death. Jason found it amusing to be a constant thorn in the old woman's side. Franky tried to help her out whenever he could, which often included smacking Jason upside his little head.

"Whatchu doing out here talking about people?" Franky asked.

"I'm just playing with that girl with the stinky breath. It's too late in the day to have stinky breath. That's supposed to be in the morning time," he said, fanning his nose.

Franky laughed and shook his head at the little boy.

"It is," Jason said with wide eyes. "It seems like it would've gone away by now. She needs to eat some candy."

"Then she'll have rotten teeth like the ones you have."

"I ain't got no rotten teeth," Jason said, spreading his lips to show off his crooked teeth.

" 'Ain't got'? What kind of way is that for you to be talking when you just left school?" Franky snapped. "It's 'I don't have any rotten teeth.' "

"Whatever. I don't wanna talk white," Jason said.

"So doing something right makes you white?" Franky asked. "Where'd you get that nonsense from?"

Jason shrugged.

"Boy, you shouldn't say things you can't explain. Don't be a follower," Franky said. "How was school today?"

"It was good."

"What color are you on?" Franky asked, referring to the color-coded behavior chart that told the kids' parents if their child had a good, okay, or bad day. Green signaled good, yellow meant okay, and red equaled bad.

"Green," Jason said with a huge smile.

"Yeah, right," Franky said with an exaggerated frown. "Let me see it."

Jason walked over to the window and dropped his book bag on the ground. He leaned down to retrieve his folder and held it up for Franky to see a big green smiley face.

"Coooooooool. That's what's up, lil whoadie," Franky said. "I'm proud of ya."

"I told you. Now, whatchu gonna give me?"

"I'ma give you a chance to keep your teeth. How about that?"

"Maaaan," Jason said, sucking his teeth. "Tomorrow I'ma get on red. Just because of you."

"Go ahead and I'ma give you a black eye to match it.

You gonna be looking just like them Jordans you're wearing. How about that?"

"Then you going to jail for child abruse."

Franky chuckled at his young friend's butchering of the English language. "It's child *abuse,* not *abruse.*"

"Whatever. My teacher said she's gonna give me some candy if I stay on green, but I need some money, man."

"What are you gonna do with money? You're six years old."

"I'm seven, and I can get me some food from Mc-Donald's."

"I'll tell you what. You stay on green all week and I'll take you to McDonald's on Friday. Is that a deal?"

"Deal," Jason said, smiling from ear to ear. "What color you on?"

"I'm not on any color. I'm too old for that."

"But you ain't too old to be in school. Why don't you go to school?"

"Now you're minding my business. I'm supposed to mind yours, not the other way around, lil boy."

Jason fanned him off and pushed his folder back into his book bag. "Okay, Franky. I'll see you later, dummy," he said as he ran off.

Franky smiled as Jason ran off. His heart sank as he watched Jason begin crossing the street without even looking for cars. He quickly scanned the street to see if any vehicles were coming. Luckily the coast was clear, and his little friend made it across in one piece.

Franky turned away from the window and walked into the bathroom. He turned on the light and saw a few roaches scatter. Barely hanging on the wall over the sink was a cracked mirror, and the old sink was more rust than porcelain. He looked into the mirror and wasn't too happy with the guy he saw staring back at him.

Creamy colored skin—the product of a Caucasian mother and an African-American father—light brown eyes that bordered on hazel, and jet-black curly hair were reflected back at him. He was a lighter complexioned version of his father, and that made him very happy. At least every time he looked at himself he would see the man who meant the most to him. They had been so close, and he missed him more than words could ever express. He turned away from the mirror and walked over to the toilet to empty his bladder. Someone hadn't even bothered to flush after doing their business, and he thought that was disgusting. Unfortunately, he had long ago gotten used to being disgusted. He frowned, shook his head, then used his foot to flush the waste down into the sewer system. After he was done with his bathroom business, he washed his hands and walked out to the living room. He stood in the doorway and watched his cousins. They were doing what they did every day—nothing. Franky walked into the kitchen with hopes that something edible would've magically appeared in the refrigerator overnight. He opened the refrigerator and saw a half-finished bottle of beer, some eggs, an empty pitcher that they used for Kool-Aid, and a carton with about a half cup of milk still in it. He reached in and grabbed the carton, opened it, placed it to his lips, and drained it. He threw the empty container in the trash can and slammed the refrigerator door shut. He walked over to the cabinets and looked in them. Nothing. He closed the door and walked out into the living room.

"Well, well, well. Look who has risen from the dead,"

Rico Bourgeois, Franky's cousin, said in a heavy New Orleans drawl. Rico was short and somewhat chubby. He wore his long hair in cornrows. His teeth were covered in gold, and tattoos were everywhere on his body, but he was wasting his money because his dark skin made it difficult to make out anything. "Man, you gonna have to do something about all that sleep. You go to bed early and wake up late. Is ya pregnant, whoadie?"

"You ever see a male get pregnant? I'm hungry. When are we gonna get some food?" Franky asked.

"Food? Is that all you think about? Eating and sleeping," Rico said. "That's all you do. You don't even go outside and shoot hoops. Stay round here eating and sleeping."

"Yep, he's pregnant," Nigel, Rico's older brother, said as he pressed the Pause button on the video game to laugh at his own joke. Nigel was the opposite of Rico. No tattoos, clean white teeth, and a low, Caesar-type haircut. Yet there was no mistaking that they were brothers. They shared the same dark brown complexion, big full lips, and fat faces. Nigel had a long scar down the left side of his face—a gift from a fight in the rough-and-tumble Calliope Projects. The scar gave him a menacing look, but he was as nice as anyone could ever be. And he was the sole reason they were alive.

"Where you gonna get some money from to give Jason's lil bad butt?" Rico asked.

"I don't know," Franky said. "He ain't gonna earn it anyway, so it doesn't matter."

"Check this out," Rico said, standing up and walking in front of the small television set. "Now that we are all together, I need to share my plan witcha. We gonna make some big dough, whoadie. I've been chewing on this one for a minute now. Kept it to myself so I didn't jinx it, ya heard, but it's time to let the cat outta the bag."

"Here we go," Nigel said, already shaking his head while frantically working the video game's controller and trying to see around his little brother. Over the years, Rico had come up with some of the worst ideas known to man about how to make some money. He was a prime candidate for the show *The World's Dumbest Criminals*. He had been arrested so many times that he had lost count. One time he robbed a Payless ShoeSource right after they first opened for business. He was arrested with a grand total of nine dollars and sixty-three cents in his pockets.

"We gonna start selling clothes. Right here in the house," Rico said. "We can have our own lil ghetto Macy's up in here, ya heard."

Nigel pressed the Pause button again and gave his little brother a how-could-you-be-so-stupid look, then went back to playing his video game.

Franky sat down beside Nigel on the beat-up sofa and grabbed the other game's controller. He reached down and reset the game without even asking.

"Thanks a lot, rude boy," Nigel said, pushing Franky's head. "I guess you in a mighty big hurry to get yo butt whipped. You couldn't let me finish my game, whoadie?"

"Whatever. What's the record?" Franky asked.

"Fifty-nine to twenty-nine, player. My way," Nigel said, bragging about the record they had been keeping of wins and losses for the last month. "Twelve more games and I'm the king."

"You're already the winner. Even if I win the next twelve, I can't catch up."

"Huh?" Nigel asked, confused. He wasn't the smartest guy in the world, but he was as good as gold when it came to his word.

"Nothing," Franky said, frustrated with explaining the smallest of things to his cousins. It was as if they hadn't even gone to elementary school to learn the basics.

"So if you can't catch up, why we playing?" Nigel asked.

"Because there ain't nothing else to do. And I'm hungry, so this can keep my mind off of eating," Franky said. "When we gonna get some food?"

"Okay," Rico said. "So y'all just gonna blow me off like my idea ain't nuttin', huh? I'm telling y'all this can work. Black folks will always try to look good, whoadie. Even if we ain't got no money for food, we dress good. Look at us. We broke as a joke, but all of us be fresh to death. If we do this, then we ain't gone have no more empty refrigerators, no more raggedy TVs, no more hot nights, 'cause I'm buying an air conditioner on the first piece of profit. No more stealing that hard toilet paper from the gas station down the street and having Habib cuss me out. I'm telling y'all it's gonna be all nice up in here."

"Where we gonna get the clothes from, Rico?" Nigel asked.

"Steal 'em. How else you think we gonna get 'em?" Rico snapped, shaking his head as if his older brother were the dumbest guy in the world.

"Steal 'em from where?" Nigel asked.

"Man, I swear you were born with three and a half brain cells. From the stores where they sell 'em, Einstein."

Nigel shook his head and kept playing.

"You didn't even think I knew who Einstein is, did ya, Franky?"

"Who is he?" Franky asked, already knowing that Rico didn't have a clue.

"Some rich white man, that's who. Don't get ya head kicked in. Anyway, where you think we gonna steal 'em from, Nigel?"

"I have no idea," Nigel said.

"You think I'ma break into the factory where they stitch them up?" Rico said. "We going right up in the store and do a smash-and-grab."

"Ever hear of cameras, idiot? We'll be locked up before we make it back to the hood. Think of something else with your eleven brain cells. And hurry up, 'cause ain't no food up in here. I got 'bout seventy dollars, and the rent is due. And I gotta pay this rent in five days or we gonna be homeless."

"Call Domino's," Rico said, plopping down in a chair that had seen better days.

"No," Nigel said. "We already had Domino's four times this week. We need to eat something with some vegetables in it."

"Pizza got vegetables on it. Ain't cheese a vegetable?" Rico asked with a frown.

"Cheese? Since when did cheese become a vegetable, braincase?" Nigel asked. "I could see if you said the tomato sauce, but cheese? I want you to stop smoking whatever it is that you've been smoking today. Make this your last day, 'cause you're already dumb enough."

"Neither one of them are a vegetable. Technically tomatoes are a fruit, and cheese is not even in the equation," Franky said as he pushed the buttons on the controller to make the little football players move here and there on the small television screen.

"Leave it up to Einstein to get all deep," Rico said, fanning his hand to brush away the smell of him passing gas. He wasn't the least bit embarrassed by his flatulence or his ignorance.

"Man," Franky said, "you stink. You smell like something crawled in you and died."

Rico laughed and kept talking. "I don't care about none of that fruit or vegetable crap. I'm ordering a pizza, and we can rob the pizza guy like we always do."

"No, you ain't," Nigel said. "You always go overboard, Rico. You need to learn to leave well enough alone, boy. You keep on pushing it and you gonna get yourself ten years in prison over some pizza."

"Well, what we gonna eat?" Rico said.

"I'll run to the grocery store in a minute," Nigel said as he made a few moves in the game. "Right after I whip up on this chump."

Franky tossed the controller on the raggedy sofa after another loss.

Nigel reached over and rubbed his little cousin on his head. "There is always next time, lil whoadie," he said, smiling and throwing his hands up in victory.

Franky leaned back on the sofa. He took a deep breath and blew out about a week's worth of frustration. He took another breath and screamed at the top of his lungs.

"Man," Rico said, looking at his cousin as if he might've finally cracked. "You need to use your inside voice, whoadie."

Nigel stared at his little cousin. He knew Franky was like a fish out of water with this ghetto living. Hurricane Katrina had done a number on all of them, but he knew that Franky was affected the most. Because before the waters came and changed all of their lives, he was a rich kid living the good life out in Jefferson Parish with his parents.

"Okay. It's time to eat," Nigel said. "Franky, walk with me to the store."

"Yeah," Rico said. "You need to let off a little steam. Outside."

2

Franky and Nigel walked down the sidewalk in their Southwest Atlanta neighborhood and took in the scenery. So many people were outside that it seemed like a street party was going on. Guys were on the corners with their shirts off, talking loudly about whatever was going on in their worlds. Kids were playing on the sidewalks, and girls were walking around in groups, enjoying their days. The old people were out on their porches, shaking their heads at some of the things they heard coming out of the mouths of the kids they had watched grow from babies. Franky spoke to the midget, Shorty, who was always standing out in front of Willy's, a liquor store, begging for change.

"Times hard on the boulevard, young buck," Shorty said. "Let me hold a lil something to take the edge off."

"Can't help you today, Shorty," Nigel said as they continued on their way.

"Well, God bless you anyway," Shorty said, then turned to the next person he saw.

They passed two check-cashing joints, which stood in the place of banks; a Laundromat that was always packed; and a few more liquor stores. Kenny's Hot Wings stand had a long line, which meant Kenny was running a sale in order to get rid of the chicken wings before they spoiled.

Franky and his cousins lived in the heart of the inner city, complete with the drug addicts, young street dealers, and all other less-fortunate folks. Every day was a struggle for the majority of the residents, and it took Franky a while to get adjusted. He learned not only to accept this as his new reality, but also figured out a way to make it work for him. Ghetto folks were some of the most resilient people he had ever seen in his young life. They made a way out of no way and always kept things interesting. Like right now. He looked to his left and saw a boy riding a bicycle full speed with a lawn mower strapped to the back. Franky tapped Nigel and showed him the guy. They both shook their heads.

Nigel was Franky's biggest blessing, and no matter what, he would always be thankful to him for saving his life. When the storms came, he swam through lots of water to help folks. And once the water gave way enough for them to drive through the streets, he loaded up Franky and Rico and came to Atlanta. It was Nigel who was responsible for them having the house where they could rest their heads, and it was Nigel who put food in their bellies. When they arrived from New Orleans three years ago, they didn't know a soul in Atlanta. They slept in their car for almost two weeks. It was Nigel who carried the load for them when then-twelve-year-old Franky and fourteen-year-old Rico could only stand by helpless. Nigel had been only sixteen years old at the time, yet he found a way for them all.

He contacted a pastor at a local church who rented them a home. He lied about his age, got a fake identification card, and found a job working at a warehouse. The company stored high-end electronics for stores like Best Buy, Circuit City, and others. Everything was fine until Nigel decided to start stealing the televisions, DVD players, and whatever else he could get his hands on. After his supervisor found out about his shady side deals, Nigel was promptly fired. He was lucky the supervisor was from New Orleans and sympathized with his plight, or he would've surely done some serious jail time. Once Nigel was out of a legitimate income, he took to the streets. He had to take care of his young brother and little cousin, so he resorted to selling small amounts of marijuana and running other little hustles to keep the lights on and food on the table. After an arrest for possession, he quit selling altogether and started washing cars and doing other little odd jobs to make ends meet.

"So what's on your mind, lil cousin?" Nigel asked once they were halfway down the street. "Seems like you need to talk."

"Hey!" Franky yelled at Jason, who was out riding his bike in the middle of the street. "Bring your lil butt over here."

"Who you yelling at?" Jason said as he rolled up on a bike that was way too big for him.

"If you run in that street again without looking, I'ma try my best to break my foot off in your lil narrow tail, ya heard," Franky said.

"Okay," Jason said as stood up on the pedals and rode off. "But how you gonna catch me, dummy?"

"Yeah, okay. Keep on. Don't let it happen again, Jason," Franky said.

"That lil boy is off the chain. I guess he's the lil brother you never had, huh? With his lil bad butt. Hate to say it but that boy will probably end up in jail or worse. He's already been caught stealing like five times. The only reason he ain't in jail right now is because of his age and because Habib has a big heart and won't press charges on him," Nigel said.

"He's not bad," Franky said. "Just misunderstood. And his grandmother is too old to put the fear in him."

"And from what I see, you ain't putting no fear in him either," Nigel said. "But keep at it. He might wise up."

"Yeah. I guess I need to step my game up," Franky said, making a mental note to lay some hands on Jason for his smart mouth the next time he was close to him.

"You're like the teenage Martin Luther King. You're a dreamer, Franky. And on these streets, daydreaming can get you messed up. I've seen lil boys younger than Jason straight pop caps in fools."

Franky shook his head at the truthfulness and tragedy of his cousin's words. He walked with his eyes straight ahead, his hands in his pockets, and his heart dragging the ground. He was always on an emotional roller coaster. One minute he could be laughing and joking and then the next be wanting to cry.

"I'm tired, man," Franky said. "I can't get it out of my head that things won't ever go back to the way they were. I miss my dad, man. Just as I was getting over my mom, my dad had to die. This just isn't fair, man. How did I get here? How did we get here?"

"Life put us here, cousin. I know how you feel. I miss my dad, too," Nigel said, showing a rare sign of vulnerability. "But what can I do about it? Nothing. So we gotta keep grinding and make our own way in this world, ya heard."

"This whole thing is crazy to me. I mean, we've been down here for almost three years, and I haven't even been to school. I liked school."

"Now, you know why you haven't been to school. We tryna stay together, ya heard. If I take you up to that school, then they gonna start asking questions . . . and the next thing you know, you'll be in a group home. We family and families stay together. We get those white folks up in our business and it's over. Maybe I can get a computer from somewhere, and you can go to school online or something."

"Nah," Franky said. "I need to be around people, Nigel. Doing things people my age do—playing basketball, football, tryna get into some girl's panties."

"You can do that without going to school. Plenty lil girls running round here with hot drawers," Nigel said.

"Nah, man. I'm talking about regular girls. Girls who are about something. I need to be a part of something. Beta club, chess club, something. Anything," Franky said with a hint of desperation.

"Now, when we first got here, you was all for staying out of school. You said you was tired of it."

"So," Franky said, raising his voice to his older cousin for the first time. He and Rico fought all the time, but he had never considered getting loud with Nigel.

"What do you mean, 'so'?" Nigel asked.

"I mean, what kid likes school at my age? If you let most of us choose whether we go or not, I bet you over half of us wouldn't step foot in a classroom. I wanna go to

school, cuz, but the thing is, I'm so far behind now that I
don't know where they're gonna put me. I'm not about to
sit in class with a bunch of seventh graders. I'm supposed
to be in the ninth grade, and that's where I wanna be."

"Okay," Nigel said. "So that's why you've been walking
around like a zombie?"

"I mean . . . I don't know. Just this whole thing is crazy.
We out here living by ourselves, man. Maybe I've been in a
three-year funk, but it's just now really hitting me. I'm fifteen years old, man, and I don't do anything all day but
play video games."

"And sleep," Nigel said with a chuckle.

"Yeah, but when I wake up, I play video games and go
back to sleep. I know my mom and my dad are looking
down at me crying their eyes out. They didn't raise me like
this."

"That's the truth. Uncle Frank and Auntie had you all
nerded up," Nigel said.

"I wish I could go back to being nerded up," Franky
said. "At least I knew that I was going to eat every day and
that my life was going to be about something. Right now I
don't know. Folks around here shooting at people all day
and night. Crack addicts trying to break in the house—
man, it's crazy, and I don't like it one bit."

"Listen to me, boy," Nigel snapped. "I'm doing the best
I can. I stopped selling weed so I wouldn't get locked up
and leave you out here by yourself. So I don't need you
throwing in my face what we don't have. I'm sorry I can't
provide a big pretty house like the one Uncle and Auntie
had you in back in Nawlins, but I'm doing the best I can,
ya heard?"

Franky nodded. "Yeah, I know. I'm sorry, cuz. I didn't

mean to knock you. If it wasn't for you, I don't know where I'd be or even if'd be living."

"Yeah," Nigel said. "Sorry is right. You think you the only one hurting? I'll get you back in school, and I'll get some food in the fridge, but I can't bring back Auntie and Uncle Frank. If I could, I would, ya heard."

"What you gonna do to get the rent money?" Franky asked, trying to change the subject.

"I'ma do what I always do," Nigel said with a shrug. "I'ma figure it out."

"And what is that?" Franky asked.

"I'll figure it out," Nigel said again. "You just worry about something to tell those white folks up at the school. You're smart, so use your brain."

"I'll think of something," Franky said as they walked into the store to get some much-needed groceries.

3

Franky was fast asleep in his bed when he was startled by the sound of gunshots. The shots were too close for comfort. He heard them all the time in their neighborhood but never this close. He jumped up and ran out of his room to make sure Nigel and Rico were all right. Nigel was sleeping peacefully, spread-eagle and wearing only his boxer shorts. The gunshots didn't even make him stir. Franky backed away from his room and raced across the hallway to Rico's room. He wasn't there, but that wasn't really that unusual. Nine out of ten nights, he would be on the streets somewhere doing something he had no business doing. Franky walked back to his room and sat on the bed.

Pow! Pow! Pow!

He heard more shots. His heart began to race, and he felt helpless. He slid off of the bed onto the floor, hoping none of the bullets would find their way into his bedroom.

Pow! Pow!

He heard more shots but this time from a different type of gun. Suddenly, someone was outside of his window. As if he were watching a low-budget action film, he saw someone leap through his open bedroom window and land on the floor with a thud. Franky jumped up, ready to fight.

The boy, who was about his age, give or take a year or two, held his hands up to his mouth, signaling for Franky to be quiet.

"Man, what the . . . ," Franky said, startled to the point where he felt as if he were on the verge of a heart attack. "What do you think you are doing?"

"Please, man," the boy said with tears in his eyes. "These dudes out there tryna kill me."

"Kill you?"

"Yes. Please, man. Please. I beg you to let me stay here for a minute," the boy pleaded.

"I don't know anything about that. You gonna have to get out of here," Franky said, standing up and walking over to his bedroom door. "You can go back out of that window or use the door, but you need to leave right now."

"*Please,* man. I'm begging you. I didn't do nothing, man. I'm not a thief or anything like that, man. I work every day," the boy pleaded through his tears. "I don't wanna die, man. My momma . . . ," he said, then dropped his head. "I don't wanna die."

Franky didn't respond. He stood at the door watching the boy.

The boy popped his head up and started patting his pockets. "Here, I'll pay you." Desperation was oozing out of the boy's eyes.

Something told Franky that the boy was okay, yet he was still wary. People played all kinds of games in the hood. This wasn't some nice suburban area where you could give someone the benefit of the doubt. Franky cursed himself for leaving his window up, but the Georgia heat was making the house a sweatbox.

The boy must've read the hesitation in Franky's eyes, because he started pulling wads of money from both pockets.

"Take it. Here, take it. Just let me stay here for a few more minutes. Please," the boy whispered.

Franky heard footsteps and people talking in the back-yard. They stopped outside of his window.

"Where that fool go?" one of them said.

"I don't know. He gotta be round here somewhere," the other one replied.

"That fool got some jets on him. He must be related to Houdini or somebody."

The boy looked at Franky and held up his hands as if praying to the god of Franky.

"Frankyyyy," a voice called from outside.

"Yeah," Franky said, keeping his eye on the boy and walking over to the window. He turned away from the boy and acted as if he had been asleep. "What's up?"

"You hear anything back here?" a man with a baritone voice asked him.

Franky recognized the tone and knew right away who he was talking to: Stick.

Stick was an older guy from the neighborhood and a complete born loser. He was at least thirty-five years old, and all he did all day, every day was run around the same ten-block radius of Atlanta's west end with kids who were young enough to be his children. He still lived with his mother and was always running some kind of scam. If you wanted a hot television, DVDs, or even the latest Blu-ray players or bootleg movies, Stick was the guy to see. He even sold chicken and steaks that had been pilfered from the local supermarkets. If a neighbor wanted to have lobster for dinner, he would ask Stick and miraculously the seafood would be on his table at dinnertime.

"Nah," Franky said, wiping his eyes. All of a sudden, he felt sorry for the guy who was hiding behind him on the floor, holding his breath for fear that his attackers would hear him breathing. "Is that you out here shooting?"

"Yeah, came up on a lil lick, but the fool got away. He must be a track star or somebody, 'cause baby boy was moving. Messed up my night, 'cause I needed that money."

"Yeah, well, I'm sorry I can't help you, Stick," Franky said. "And use some silencers next time. I gotta go to school in the morning."

"School?" Stick said with a frown. "You going lame on me?"

"Yeah," Franky said.

"A'ight, lil homie," Stick said. "Take your lame tail back to bed."

"You see him?" Rico asked as he jogged up to Stick from the opposite side of the house. "Franky, you hear anybody back here?"

"Nope," Franky said, disappointed but not surprised to see that his cousin was involved in this little scheme with the likes of Stick.

"A'ight, let's walk up this way, Stick," Rico said with a big smile on his face as if they were playing a game of hide-

and-seek. "I know that fool can't be too far away, ya heard?"

Franky closed the window and walked back over to his bed. He sat down and sighed.

"Thanks, man," the boy said. "Those dudes are crazy."

"You sho right about that," Franky said.

"May I use your phone? I must've dropped mine when I was running for my life."

"We don't have a phone, whoadie," Franky said, staring at the frightened boy.

The boy grimaced and rubbed his hands over his face as if the harder he rubbed, the quicker he could come up with a solution to his current predicament.

"Here," the boy said, handing Franky the money. "A deal is a deal. You saved my life."

"What are you gonna do? You can't stay here."

"I know," the boy said. "Can you give me a little time to figure something out?"

"Might as well. You're here," Franky said with a shrug of his shoulders. "But one of those dudes . . . ," Franky started, but caught himself. He didn't know this guy, and he didn't want him returning with the police to take Rico away.

The boys sat in silence for a few minutes before Franky spoke. "Where did you get all of this money?"

"I work," the boy said. "I was over here trying to buy a car, but the guy kept giving me the runaround. Now that I think about it, it was a hustle the whole time," the boy said, shaking his head. "No wonder they kept saying bring cash. Cash only. Cash only."

Franky knew exactly the hustle he was referring to. Take a picture of a nice car, something that young people would like—a Dodge Charger, a Chevrolet Impala, or something like that—post it on a Web site that sells cars, and when the person comes to test drive it, the goons pop out. Some hustlers use a girl to distract the buyer and then they take his money.

Franky held the guy's money in his hand. He leaned over so he could see a little better, then counted the bills. He was holding three thousand dollars.

"It's like eleven o'clock at night. Why would you come to buy a car this time of night, in this neighborhood? Do you have a death wish? Or maybe you just wanna be robbed," Franky asked.

"Nah. I just got off work. I jumped straight on the MARTA," the boy said, shaking his head. "Wow. I could be dead right now."

"Yes, you could," Franky said, handing the boy back his money and standing up. "But you are not, so go home."

The boy held his hand up and refused the money.

"Here," Franky said, pushing the money to his chest. "Take your money."

The boy took a deep breath, then reached out for his cash.

"Just be a little more careful next time," Franky said.

"Man, can I give you some of it? You don't know what you did for me."

"Yes, I do," Franky said, walking out of the room and leading the guy to the front door. "But I would want somebody to do the same thing for me. Take care, whoadie."

"Man," the boy said, looking around when Franky opened the front door. "My name is Davante. I'm not going to forget this. I have to give you something. Here," he said, peeling off about half the bills and handing them to Franky.

"I already told you that I'm good, but since you insist that I take your money, then fine," Franky said, thinking about the empty refrigerator, the bare cabinets, and the past-due rent as he took the wad of bills.

"I'ma come back by here and . . . I don't know what I'm going to do, but I wanna let you know I appreciate this," Davante said.

"Don't sweat it, whoadie," Franky said.

Davante reached out his hand, and Franky shook it. "Be careful out there, ya hear?"

"Yeah," Davante said. He stepped out on the porch and looked around one last time before he took off running.

Franky watched him as he ran straight down the sidewalk without looking back.

The entire ordeal was crazy, but what bothered Franky the most was how normal he felt. He turned around, walked back to his room, and sat down on the bed. He counted his loot and smiled. He was six hundred dollars richer. He stashed the money in his sneaker and lay down on the bed. Before five minutes had passed, he was fast asleep.

4

The alarm clock sounded and Franky's eyes popped open. He jumped up and almost ran to the bathroom to get his morning shower. Today was a school day—the first time he would attend school in almost three years. He was nervous and excited all at the same time. After his shower, he went back to his room and got dressed. He slipped his slender body into some crisp Levi's and a blue-and-white-striped Polo shirt that fit nice and snug, and then put on his navy-blue Air Max 95s. He wondered how it would feel being back in a classroom after all these years of being stagnant.

"Franky," Nigel said as he walked into his cousin's bedroom. "Where did you get this money?"

"It should cover the rent, right?" Franky said, looking into the mirror as he brushed his hair.

"Yeah, but where'd you get it from?" Nigel asked again.

"I found it," Franky lied.

"When?"

"Just now."

"Where did you find three hundred dollars just now, Franky?" Nigel asked, as if he were a stern father.

"In the backyard. I looked out the window and saw it on the ground," Franky said with a wide smile. "Why you giving me the third degree?"

" 'Cause I don't want you round here doing nothing you don't have no business doing, ya heard," Nigel said.

"Well, I looked out the window just like I do every morning. I saw that money, and I jumped out there and got it. Don't complain. Just be happy we can pay the rent," Franky said.

"Boy, you better be glad I know that you haven't left this house," Nigel said. "This is just too good to be true. Don't nobody just leave three hundred dollars lying around."

"You say you found that in the backyard?" Rico asked as he walked into Franky's room.

"Yep," Franky said as he continued to brush his hair as if the curls were going to straighten up. "Hey, Nigel, I need some school supplies. Can we run to the store and get some paper and pencils before I go to school? I don't wanna show up looking like I don't have a clue."

"How much money did you find, Franky?" Rico asked, staring at his cousin with a squinted eye.

"Three hundred dollars," he said. "I gave it to Nigel."

"That's my money, whoadie," Rico snapped.

"How?" Franky asked, finally stopping the brushing.

" 'Cause it is," Rico said. "Now give it up."

"You lost some money outside in the backyard?" Nigel asked his brother.

"Nah," Rico said as he walked up on his little cousin.

Franky was taller, but he was a bag of bones. Rico was short, compact, and strong as an ox. "And it wasn't no three hundred dollars—it was three thousand dollars, so where the rest at?"

"What?" Franky said, feeling a little threatened.

"You heard me," Rico growled.

"Man," Franky said, "I don't know what in the world you're talking about. If I found three thousand dollars, I wouldn't be asking Nigel to buy me some school supplies. I could buy 'em myself."

"Yeah, you would," Rico said as he slung open the closet and started throwing Franky's clothes out. " 'Cause you think you're smarter than everybody. You think you Einstein. Now where the money at?" Rico yelled.

"Hey," Nigel barked at his brother. "Cut it out and put those clothes back in his closet. What's wrong with you?"

"Nah," Rico said. "This fool holding out, and I want my money."

"Rico," Nigel said in a low and threatening tone. "I'm not going to tell you again."

Rico continued to pull things out of drawers and closets as if Nigel was talking to the wall. Nigel went to his room and left Franky alone with Rico the madman. He stood watching his cousin, and it was as if something evil had taken over his body.

"Empty your pockets," Rico said, turning to Franky, his chest rising and falling as air fought to get into his lungs.

"Rico, you trippin'," Franky said, pulling out his empty pockets.

"Take your shoes off," Rico said.

Nigel walked back in the room with a baseball bat. "Rico," he said. "You are my little brother and I love you, but if you don't get out of here right now with all this foolishness, I'ma try my best to Barry Bonds yo head across this room."

"This fool playing games, ya heard," Rico snapped. "He holding out, and it's my money."

"First of all, he paid the rent, which is more than you've ever done in all the time we been here. Second of all, how is it your money?"

" 'Cause me and Stick had this fool set up last night. One of those car-sale deals. Old boy took off running. He must've dropped the money while he was getting up outta here. And he had three thousand dollars, not three hundred." Rico poked his finger at Franky's skinny chest.

"So you think because you and Superdummy's plan didn't work out and the dude got away that you are owed some money?"

"Yeah," Rico said with a straight face. "If he dropped the money, then it's mine."

"And what makes you think he dropped all three thousand dollars? Why couldn't he just drop three hundred?" Nigel asked.

" 'Cause he didn't and Franky holding out," Rico said, glaring at Franky.

"No, I'm not," Franky said, on the verge of tears. "I gave everything I found to Nigel so we wouldn't be put out on the street."

"Man," Nigel said, dismissing his brother. "Clean this boy's room back up. I swear you gotta be the dumbest dude I know. If you weren't my brother, I'd knock you across your head for this. Now, you know Franky ain't even like that, and even if he was, you missed your lick. Get over it."

"I'll clean it up when I get home. I don't want him all in my stuff," Franky said.

" 'Cause you holding out, and you know I'll find it," Rico said. "Go on. Take your lil lame butt to school. I'll have all the time I need while you're up there getting your brain worked on."

"Even if you find it, it's not yours, idiot," Nigel said. "But I know you better not step foot in this boy's room."

"Yeah," Rico said. "Picture that."

"Get out," Nigel said, walking up to Rico. All bets were off now, and Franky knew that Rico was about to get a major beat-down. Rico must've known it, too, because he put his hands up and backed out of the room. "And don't you come back in here no more. This is Franky's room. I don't go in your room, so you stay out of his. Let's go, Franky."

Franky looked at the mess of clothes that his cousin had thrown everywhere and shook his head.

He could toss the room upside down and he wouldn't find the other three hundred dollars, because it was stashed in the handle of his brush, which he just slid into his back pocket.

"Rico, man," Franky said. "That's messed up what you did to my room and what you accused me of. You know I'm not a thief. If it was your money, I would've given it to you, but I gave it to Nigel to help pay the rent."

"Yeah," Rico said, frowning his chubby face up. "Well, if you telling the truth, then I'm sorry, but if you lying, I'll find out and I'ma whip that butt. Have fun in school."

"If I find out you been in this room," Nigel said, "there's gonna be some serious consequences for you, and you won't have to worry about whipping no butt, ya heard?"

Rico nodded. He couldn't go against his big brother and win. He gave Franky the evil eye and walked to his room.

"I gave you everything I had," Franky said to Nigel with a straight face. He had plans for the other money. He wouldn't be hungry again. That other three hundred dollars was for when his ribs threatened to kiss his back, and although Nigel always made a way, he was getting tired of living like that. The three hundred dollars was his insurance of always having a meal.

"I believe you. And even if you didn't, so what. Let's get you to school."

5

Favorite civil rights icons Martin Luther King Jr. and Malcolm X were shaking hands. The one and only time they ever met was forever bronzed and standing tall out in front of the school named to honor them. Malcolm Martin High School was huge, and once Franky was inside, he was tempted to turn around. The place was so chaotic that for some strange reason it reminded him of a jail more than a school.

Before Franky and Mrs. Bertha could enter the building, they had to walk through a metal detector that was manned by two buff guys wearing tight-fitting uniforms complete with full pistol belts. Franky looked down at the belt of one of the guards and saw two sets of handcuffs, two cans of pepper spray, and one big black pistol. He looked past the metal detector and saw two more uniformed officers walking with two large German shepherds who were sniffing lockers and students as they walked by.

What in the world have I gotten myself into? Franky wondered.

Then there was another shocker. Everywhere he turned, he saw black faces, and they were loud and wild and unruly. Try as he might, he couldn't find one white face in the crowd of what seemed like a million and one kids running around screaming and yelling. He even saw two kids fighting as people walked by as if nothing was out of the ordinary. Maybe this was ordinary, he thought. This was truly an all-black school. The teachers were black, the kids were black, the janitors were black, the security guards were black, and even the drug-sniffing dogs were black.

At every school Franky had ever attended since he was a mere six months old, he had always been in the minority, and he'd never even stepped foot in a public school. He had gotten so accustomed to being the one of two or three blacks in school that Malcolm Martin High School was a complete culture shock. Even though he grew up in New Orleans, he had never really been a part of black New Orleans.

You from New Orleans. We from Nawlins, Rico used to tease.

Finally, he knew what he meant. This new school environment was going to take some getting used to. But he was here now, and he might as well get started. Nigel had asked Mrs. Bertha if she'd register Franky into the school. She was perfect for the job. She was old and wasn't really in the right frame of mind to answer too many probing questions. They had their story down, which wasn't that far off from the truth. Franky had come up from New Orleans after the storms in which he lost both of his parents and was trying to find new traction in a new city. After a three-year battle with depression, he was finally ready to move on with his life. They even practiced what they would say if the school officials asked certain questions, but they were pleasantly surprised when the nice lady behind the desk didn't dig too deep. She said they had an influx of people from New Orleans, and special arrangements were made for the displaced.

"What grade did you last complete, Franky?" Mrs. Bromfield, the school's registrar and secretary, asked.

"Sixth," he answered honestly. "But I—"

"Don't worry about it. We'll test you and see where you fit in," she said, reading the worried expression on Franky's face.

"He's a smart boy," Mrs. Bertha said. "Just been through a lot in his young life."

"I understand," Mrs. Bromfield said, nodding sympathetically at Franky. "I can only imagine. You'll have ninety days to get us a copy of his birth certificate, but if you need more time, just let us know."

"Okay," Mrs. Bertha said.

Franky wasn't sure how he was going to go about obtaining any of his records, but he had time to figure it out. Right now he was only interested in hearing that he could stay in high school.

"When can I take the test? I was already reading three levels above my class at my last school. And I was taking algebra in sixth grade," he bragged.

"That's great," Mrs. Bromfield said. "You will be fine. What is the name of the last school you attended?"

"Jimrose Academy," he said. "It's a private school in New Orleans."

"Thank you," Mrs. Bromfield said as she tapped away at her computer. "I'm sure this is a far cry from that, but it'll be what you make it, Mr. Bourgeois. Some of our kids do very well academically and others not so good. It's all about the work you put in and the people you associate with. I tell everyone who walks through that door—association breeds assimilation. You hang with scholars, then more than likely you will be a scholar. If you hang with nutcases, well . . . more than likely you'll be a nutcase. Pretty simple, don't you think?"

"Yes, ma'am," Franky said.

He looked over at Mrs. Bertha, who only nodded at him as if to say he was doing fine.

"Here is your schedule and your locker number and combination. You will use these numbers right for your lunch. There is a little box at the end of the line. You'll see what I mean when you get there," she said, pointing at the top of his page. "Now, if you will have a seat in that chair."

Franky sat in the chair situated in front of a white background. Mrs. Bromfield came out with a camera and pointed it at him. "Say cheese," she said, snapping the picture. "Now, if you will fill out this information, I will get your identification card ready."

"When do I take the test?" Franky asked.

"You will take the placement exam no later than Friday, and once we get your scores back, we may or may not change your classes," Mrs. Bromfield said.

"Okay," Franky said, taking in all of the information.

"Right now you are taking basic freshman classes. Good luck. Oh," Mrs. Bromfield said. "I almost forgot. Do you need a bus schedule?"

I wouldn't dare get on one of those cheese buses, he thought.

"No, ma'am. We live only a few blocks away. I can walk," Franky said, taking the paper and standing up.

"Well, Franky, you seem to be a very bright young man. Don't let anyone influence you to change that," Mrs. Bromfield said before handing him his identification card and reaching out to shake his hand. "Good luck, but I'm sure you'll do well."

"Thanks," Franky said, shaking her hand. "I'm looking forward to it."

"Make sure you wear your ID at all times. If you lose it, you'll need to come see me right away. The security guards are pretty strict about not letting kids in without them."

Franky walked over and helped Mrs. Bertha to her feet. She was a heavy woman, and she seemed to put all of her weight on his bony legs as she stood. He led her over to the door and out of the office. They headed down the hallway, past the black German shepherd, past the metal detectors, and out the front door of the old building.

Nigel was standing on the front steps of the school building waiting for them. "You all set?" he asked with a smile once they stepped outside.

"Yeah! They're putting me in ninth-grade classes," Franky said with a huge, infectious smile. "But the lady said I have to take a few tests before they'll know for sure."

"That shouldn't be a problem for you, Einstein," Nigel teased. "I'm glad things are working out. We should've done this a long time ago. But it is what it is, right?"

"It's all good," Franky said, swatting his cousin's guilt

away like a fly. "Man, it's like a zoo up in there. I've never seen anything like that in my life. Those kids are buck wild. They are screaming and cussing and everything else, and the adults don't even say anything. I'm telling you, cuzzo. It's crazy."

"Welcome to public schools in the hood," Nigel said with a shrug. "You'll be fine. Stand tall and don't let nobody punk you, ya heard. Somebody try to swing at you, you make sure you send a message to anybody else who might wanna follow them. I mean, you try your best to break something. I got your back, ya heard?"

"Yeah," Franky said, confused. Was he going to prison or school? He couldn't help but think back to the last time he was in school and how gravely different this pep talk was from his mother's.

Franky, make sure you sit in the front of the class and pay close attention. Take good notes and always do your best. Have a great day, son. I love you.

Franky's parents were all about education, and they preached to him about the importance of being black and educated. They pushed him to do his best in every class. If he ever struggled in a class, they hired a tutor. Now here was his cousin telling him to swing for the fences with his fist. The word *study* never came out of his mouth.

"A'ight, well, I better get back in there and find these classes," Franky said. "Thanks for everything, Mrs. Bertha."

"No, chile," she said. "Thank you. I love to hear young black boys acting like they got some sense. I'm eighty-six years old, and I marched with Dr. King, and it wasn't easy. We got hit with rocks and all kinds of things, but we believed that black schools should be just as nice as the white ones. Now look how we act. Dr. King must be turning flips in his grave over the way our people are down here carrying on."

As if on cue to validate Mrs. Bertha's words, two girls walked by, both with red and blue hair and shorts so short they should be outlawed, calling each other the B word.

Mrs. Bertha shook her head. "Shameful. But, Franky, I'm proud of you," she said. "I swear I think you put a few more years on my life. There is hope after all."

"That's good to hear. We need you around. Who else is going to make sure we get a nice Sunday meal each week?" Franky said with a smile as he helped the old lady down the twenty or so steps that led up to the school.

Once they had Mrs. Bertha situated in the passenger seat of the same old car that brought the boys from New Orleans, Nigel walked around to the driver's side and got in. He threw the peace sign to his cousin and pulled off.

"Yo, boi," a familiar voice said from across the yard as Franky walked back toward the school. He turned around and noticed two guys from his neighborhood, Bubba and Bernard.

Bubba was already six feet three inches tall and was about one hundred and ninety pounds of pure muscle. The fact that he was only in ninth grade had every AAU basketball coach in the city vying for his services. He was a beast on the basketball courts and wasn't anything to sneeze at on the gridiron, but there was something about the street life that had his nose wide open.

Nard was the complete opposite of Bubba. He was short, fat, and had already been held back to give the ninth grade another try. He was also throwing rocks at the penitentiary, begging for them to let him in. His mother was a drug addict, and there was never any mention of a father. He was angry at the world for dealing him a bad deck of cards. In order for him to feel good about himself, he bullied smaller and weaker kids and was always on the prowl for his next victim. Franky tried to keep his distance from him, but now that they attended the same school, that wasn't going to be as easy anymore.

"What y'all doing out here?" Franky asked for lack of having anything else to say.

" 'Bout to go get something to grub on," Nard said. "You roll?"

"Nah," Franky said. "This is my first day here. I'm not about to skip. What's up, Bubba?"

"What's good with ya, boi?" Bubba said as he walked over to Franky and gave him a brotherly hug. "So you up here now, huh?"

"Yeah, man," Franky said. "It's about time. Tired of sitting around that house all day, ya heard."

"I feel ya," Bubba said. "We got basketball tryouts today. You coming?"

"Nah," Franky said. "I can't shoot that rock. I'm a football kind of guy."

"You a'ight," Bubba said. "You'll make the team if I tell Coach to pick you."

"Why you ain't tell him to pick me for the lil b-ball squad?" Nard asked.

" 'Cause you suck. At least Franky can ball a lil bit. Plus, they ain't got no uniforms that wide," Bubba teased.

"Oh, you think that's funny, Franky?" Nard snapped.

Franky laughed as he imagined Nard's fat body wobbling up and down a basketball court. "Yeah," Franky said. "That was hilarious."

"Man, y'all always clowning. Anyway, I'm hungry. Come

on, man. Roll with us. We'll be back before it's time to go to class. The late bell ain't gonna ring for a few," Nard said.

"Y'all go ahead," Franky said. "I'll see y'all when y'all get back."

"Okay, lame boi," Nard said, staring Franky up and down to see what his response to the slight diss would be.

"I got your lame right here," Franky said, grabbing his genitals and thinking about his cousin's warning.

Sensing that this little situation could escalate into something bigger, Bubba stepped in. "A'ight, boi," Bubba said, reaching out to shake Franky's hand. "We'll holla atcha later. I'll see you around. Hold up a second. Who you got next period?"

Franky looked at his schedule and ran his finger down the paper to see who his teacher was. "Mrs. White, I think. Next period is third, right? I missed the first two getting registered."

"Yeah, Mrs. White is cool. Let me see if we got any classes together," Bubba said, scanning the paper.

"We're together for first period, but that's about all. They got you in the slow classes, brah."

"Slow classes?" Franky asked. "I need to get that changed, then."

"Well, they're not slow as in special ed, but the people you with ain't the sharpest knives in the drawer. If you know what I mean," Bubba said, sneaking a look at Nard.

"Aww, man," Franky said as the wind left his sails.

"We got physical ed with Coach English. He's the football coach. He's cool, too, but he don't play," Bubba said.

"A'ight, man. I'll holla atcha, lady, whoadie," Franky said, still pissed about being with the slow kids.

"A'ight, boi, we out," Bubba said.

Franky slapped Bubba's hand and winked at Nard.

"Don't let your mouth write a check that your lil narrow butt can't cash, boi," Nard said with a sinister snarl, showing the top half of his gold-covered teeth.

"Yeah, I'll remember that," Franky said as he turned around and walked back up the steps for his first official day of high school.

6

"Thank you, Mrs. Bertha," Nigel said as he parked on the street in front of their house. "We appreciate you doing that for us. And you know to call us if you need anything. One of us will be right there for you."

"Oh, no problem. Y'all some sweet boys. I don't mind at all," Mrs. Bertha said as she got out of the car. She grunted and huffed until she was up and out of the car. She stepped onto the sidewalk and took a deep breath as if that alone was taking the wind out of her.

Nigel noticed the front curtain move in the old woman's house, and he could've sworn he saw a figure behind it.

"Mrs. Bertha," he said, staring hard at the curtain. "Is anybody in your house?"

"Better not be," she said, fiddling around in her purse for her door keys as she walked up her driveway.

"Do you mind sitting tight for a minute?" Nigel asked. "I think I just saw something move in your house. I hope my eyes are playing tricks on me, but I wanna be sure."

Mrs. Bertha frowned. "Oh, don't say that. Here," she said, handing her keys to Nigel. "You go on in there and check it out for me. I'm too old for surprises."

Nigel walked up on the porch and opened the screen door. He could hear footsteps inside. Someone was definitely in the woman's house. And he was pissed that he didn't have any kind of weapon on him. He took a deep breath before unlocking the door. He had no idea what he was walking into, but he would rather it be him than Mrs. Bertha. He pushed open the door just in time to see Stick running down the hallway with something in his hands.

"Hey!" Nigel said as loud as he could. "Get out of here."

He halfheartedly ran after the neighborhood superbum as Stick made his getaway out the back door. Nigel quickly walked through the other rooms to see if Stick had an accomplice. Once satisfied that the coast was clear, he turned around and walked back outside.

"Mrs. Bertha," he said. "I just saw somebody run out of your back door. You should call the police."

"Oh, Lord," she said, walking up toward her house. "I gotta move from round here. I'm too old for this mess. People just ain't respectful no more."

"Yeah," Nigel said, feeling bad for the old woman who had been nothing short of an angel to them since they moved in. "It's pretty bad around here."

Mrs. Bertha walked into her house and went straight to her bedroom. She was gone only a few seconds before walking back out to the living room carrying an empty wooden box. The pained and defeated expression on her face bothered Nigel.

"They took my husband's watches. He left those watches

for Jason," she said, shaking her head. "He got those things when he was in the war, and he was so proud of them."

Mrs. Bertha plopped down on the sofa, her chin on her chest and the empty box sitting on her lap. She reached up and pulled the wig off her head and sighed. She looked up at Nigel with tears in her eyes. "Lord, what happened to my people?"

Nigel felt like someone had robbed his own grandmother. He understood the streets were a cold place to be, but old ladies were always off-limits. They were walking angels, and he couldn't tolerate anyone who would cause them any harm. He made a mental note to kick Stick's head into the ground the next time he saw him.

"I will look around and see if I can find out who broke into your house. Maybe I can even get your stuff back," Nigel said, but the old lady was wailing loud now. Seeing her like this broke his heart into a million tiny pieces.

Mrs. Bertha rocked herself back and forth. She was in a daze now, and she mumbled what Nigel believed to be her dead husband's name over and over.

Nigel walked out of the woman's house and ran across the street to his own place.

"Rico," he called out. "Rico."

Rico wasn't answering, and the fact that he was gone pissed him off even more than he already was. That meant he was probably with Stick when they broke into Mrs. Bertha's house. Nigel opened the door to Franky's room and noticed that all of his little cousin's belongings were on the floor.

"That boy has lost his mind," he said to himself. "Not only did he come in this room after I told him not to, but also I'll bet he was in that woman's house with Stick. That's two heads I need to crack."

Nigel grabbed his baseball bat and ran out of his house just in time to see a black and white police car pull onto his street. The officer didn't look his way as he sped by, and he ignored the officer. His sights were on the ugly yellow house at the end of the street. He walked up the driveway leading to Stick's house and took the steps two at a time. He knocked on the door and waited. He placed his ear a little closer to the door that had seen better days and heard a television. He knocked again.

"Yo, Stick. Open this door, man," he said.

A few seconds later, the door jingled and then opened. Before he could say anything to Stick, Nigel turned around to see an ambulance flying down his street toward Mrs. Bertha's house.

"What's up with ya, playboy?" Stick said with his usual raggedy-toothed smile, as if they were old buddies.

"You see what you did?" Nigel said, pointing at the ambulance. He opened the screen door and walked into the house without waiting for an invite.

"Whoa, whoa, whoa. Slow your roll, playboy," Stick said, no longer smiling. "Don't be coming up in here with all that. You don't know me like that."

"Where's the stuff you took?"

"I don't know what you talking about, playboy," Stick said, rubbing his beard. "I ain't never took nuttin' from nobody in my life. I'm a good, God-fearing man."

"Man, I saw you," Nigel said, "so give it up."

"Saw who? Man, I been in here sleeping all day. Done missed two episodes of *Judge Mathis* and *The Price Is Right*. My momma will vouch for that. Want me to go get her so you can ask her?" he said with a straight face.

"I'm not the police," Nigel said. "But I do know that old lady never bothered nobody, and I'm not letting you have this one, you heard?"

"Like I said, I've been up here sleep," Stick said, sticking to his story. "And if you don't mind, I'd like to go back. I think it's time for you to leave, playboy."

Nigel shook his head. What a waste of a human life. This guy was the worst sorry excuse for a man he'd ever seen. He was almost forty years old and still living at home, but to make matters worse, he was using his mother as an alibi so that he could continue his dirty deeds.

"Now you know I'm not leaving here without that lady's stuff, right? So how you wanna do this, Stick?" Nigel said, taking the bat and hitting his free hand with it.

"Like I said. Slow your roll, playboy," Stick said. "Tell you what. I'll give you a lil piece of the action. Just calm down. No need to get violent. I'm a peaceful brother. That's the problem with us—we always wanna fight each other. Can't we all just get along?"

Nigel thought about the man's proposition and decided to take a different approach. "You're right. My bad." His demeanor instantly changed from menacing to calm. "Where is Rico?"

"There ya go, playboy. See," the bum said with his hands spread wide. "Stick ain't selfish. I don't mind sharing the wealth with my people. If you come at me right, then I come at you right," Stick said, falling for Nigel's change of heart.

"I see. What was I thinking?" Nigel said. "I got a lot on my mind. Where is my brother?"

"I ain't seen Rico today," Stick said as he walked toward the back of the house and motioned for Nigel to follow him. "We had a lil lick last night that didn't work out too well. Ran my old car scam on this young buck, but the fool got away. He had some wheels on him, boy. You should've seen that joker get out. We wasn't catching him. Then your crazy brother had to go and start shooting. Walking around like we in the wild, wild west or something. I ain't fooling with him no more. He's too reckless, and like I said, I'm a peaceful brother."

"Yeah, he's a handful," Nigel said as he followed Stick to the back porch of the house.

Stick walked over to an old freezer and opened it up. He reached in and grabbed a white pillowcase that he had just taken from Mrs. Bertha's house. It was the same one Nigel had just seen him run with. He tossed the pillowcase to Nigel and smiled.

"You can go through there and get a few things to pawn. That'll put a lil money in your pocket," Stick said as if he was doing Nigel a huge favor. "I'm a generous guy if you come at me right."

"Easy to be generous when you're not giving away your own things," Nigel said, taking the case and slinging it over his shoulder. "I'm taking this back to Mrs. Bertha. This stuff don't mean jack to you, Stick—it's just another hustle. But to her this is everything. These are things her dead husband left her and Jason. He's dead now, so he can't just run out and replace them, ya heard. Do you get that?"

Stick stood there with a mean scowl on his face, but he was a coward, and he wouldn't dare make a move toward the man in front of him. Even though he had about fifteen years on Nigel, he didn't want any part of him. Nigel's words had no real effect on him other than the fact that he just lost out on another hustle. Stick stood there huffing and puffing, and Nigel couldn't help but want to punch him in the face.

"Oh, okay. You got it. Go on and take the old woman her stuff back, man. But you know that's messed up, don't you? I've been watching that house for years, and when I finally catch her leaving, you go mess it up. That's 'bout a good ten grand you holding there, but I'ma let you have it."

"You ain't gonna let me have jack," Nigel said. "I'ma let your head stay on your shoulders, so say thank you."

Stick fanned him off.

"I said say thank you," Nigel said, dropping the pillowcase onto the floor and lifting his bat into a swinging position.

"Thanks," Stick mumbled, but then got loud. "You're good but please don't mention my name. It's too hot to be locked up."

Nigel tightened his grip on his baseball bat and was tempted to have a little batting practice with Stick's cranium but decided it would be a waste of his energy. Stick was a bum and was always going to be one.

"I want you to stay out of my line, ya heard? You see me, go the other way. Do that and you'll be okay. If you don't"—Nigel made a swinging motion with his bat—"ain't no telling what I might do, ya heard?"

Stick nodded. He knew his place in the street hierarchy. He was a bottom feeder, the lowest man on the totem pole, and he was okay with that.

"Gone on, man. Take the bag," Stick said.

Nigel picked up the pillowcase and walked out of the back door, hoping that Stick would heed his advice. He didn't have a lot of patience when it came to his kind.

Once he was around Stick's house and back on the street, he saw the paramedics loading Mrs. Bertha into the back of the ambulance and couldn't help but wonder if she was going to be okay. He thought about little Jason and what he would do if something happened to his grandmother.

"Freeze," a police officer said, pointing his gun directly at Nigel. "Drop the bag and get on your knees."

Nigel froze. He dropped the bag and held his hands up above his head. He went down to his knees with his hands still in the air. He knew he was in trouble. Here he was literally holding the bag, and he knew that he would never tell on Stick. As sorry of a human being as Stick was, Nigel wasn't the type of guy to tell the police anything.

A police officer rushed over and pushed him facedown onto the hard, hot concrete.

7

Franky was running late. He had gotten confused on which hallway his classes were on two times already. Now he found himself running to get to his last class before the late bell rang. He looked down at his schedule, then up at the numbers above the wooden doors.

"Finally," he said as he heard the bell sound just as he opened the classroom door.

Franky walked in, and only a handful of students paid him any mind as he looked around for a place to sit. Four of the six chairs on the front row were free, so he walked over and took the one closest to the window.

"Good afternoon," Mr. Johnson, his teacher, said. He looked to be in his midtwenties and from first appearances seemed to be a sharp guy.

"Good afternoon," Franky said. "Is it all right if I sit here?"

"Sure," Mr. Johnson said. "I love it when students sit in the front of the class. It sends a message to the world that they're about their business."

"Suck-up," someone from the rear said, causing the peanut gallery to laugh.

"Don't pay him any attention, Mr. . . . ?"

"Franky Bourgeois."

"Nice. Is that Creole?" the teacher asked.

"French but . . . ," Franky said, hunching his shoulders.

"Okay. Well, welcome to Spanish. Take a seat and let's get started," Mr. Johnson said. "Everyone settle down and grab a paper and pencil. It's note time. There will be a test on what is on this board, so I suggest you get to writing."

Franky looked around and hardly anyone moved. He couldn't believe what he was seeing. The room itself resembled any other classroom he'd ever been in. There was a whiteboard, a podium, lots of posters on the walls with math equations, a lot of desks that were filled with teenagers, and a teacher standing at the head of the room. But that was where the similarities stopped. The entire day had been one big eye-opening experience and explained why the have-nots continue not to have. His dad used to tell him about this, but he really didn't have any real idea what he was talking about until now. Now he could see why his parents tried so hard to keep him away from the hood.

The world doesn't need another shiftless Negro, his dad would often lecture. *There are people out there who look just like you and I who will make sure the prisons stay filled because they refuse to educate themselves. I'm going to make sure you're not one of them.*

There were almost thirty kids in each of his classes, and he could count on one hand the number of them who showed the slightest amount of interest in learning what the teacher was attempting to teach. This new school would definitely take some getting used to.

Mr. Johnson, the enthusiastic Spanish teacher, was from a small town in South Carolina called Pamplico. As a child, he had always been fascinated with the foreign people he saw on television and wanted to learn how to communicate with them. Having parents who dropped out of school before they made it to high school, he made sure he studied hard and earned an academic scholarship to the University of Georgia. He finished his master's degree in Madrid, Spain. He always stressed to his students the importance of learning a second language, but as he stood at the front of the class writing sentences on the board, the majority of the class did their own thing.

The girl who sat beside Franky was texting someone on her cell phone and laughing to herself at whatever response she was getting. Every now and then, she would look at him and blow a bubble from the wad of gum she was furiously working. One chair over from her sat a little guy who looked like he should still be in elementary school. He was asleep and snoring so loud it was amazing that *he* could sleep through it. A couple of kids in the back were listening to their iPods as if they didn't have a care in the world. Two other guys were battling each other with raps while a third guy made beats with his mouth. And this was one of the calmer classes.

Mr. Johnson turned around and looked at the sleeping boy and huffed as if the snoring was just too much for him to take. He put his marker down and walked over to the boy. He stopped right beside him, leaned down right above the boy's ear, and slapped both of his hands together as loud as he could.

CLAP!

The sleeping boy didn't budge, which sent the entire

class into a laughing frenzy. Even Mr. Johnson chuckled and shook his head.

"Is he dead?" one of the kids asked.

"Have you ever heard a dead man snore?" Mr. Johnson replied.

"I don't know what midgets do when they die," the boy said.

"Come here, Mark," Mr. Johnson said to the boy. "Grab his legs and I'll get his shoulders. This is ridiculous."

Mark was tall and wore a pair of gray sweatpants, a T-shirt with M&M HIGH BASKETBALL across the front, and a pair of Nike flip-flops. He walked up, and they politely lifted the sleeping boy up from his desk and carried him outside the classroom and into the hallway. Mark decided to drop the boy's legs before Mr. Johnson could get him on the floor.

"Oops," Mark said.

"Why did I even bother asking you to help me?" Mr. Johnson said, shaking his head.

"Hey," Sleepy said, finally waking up and pulling away from Mr. Johnson. "What y'all doing to me?"

"You will not sit up in my class and sleep. Especially not as loud as you snore. Go to the office," Mr. Johnson said.

"I wasn't asleep. Man, y'all need to stop trippin'," Sleepy protested.

"What happened? You had a bug in your eye, and you were trying to suffocate it?" Mark said.

"Shut up, Mark," Sleepy said with a frown. "You so black you blend in with the dark."

"And yo momma had liquor in her titties and stunted your growth, you lil ugly bastard," Mark said.

"Hey, you guys, cut it out," Mr. Johnson said, stopping

the two before things got heated. "Mark, go in the class-room, and, Antonio, you go to the principal's office. And when you get home today, I want you to ask your mother or father to take you to see a doctor," Mr. Johnson said as he walked back into the classroom, shaking his head.

"Man, Mr. Johnson, you're a hater," Antonio said before walking down the hallway.

Franky was busy writing notes from the board when Mr. Johnson walked over and peeked at his tablet. "Thank God somebody actually wants to learn up in here," he said, and went back to the board. "I appreciate that, Mr. Bourgeois."

"Give him some time. He's new," Mark said. "We'll have him corrupted in no time."

"Sit down, Mark," Mr. Johnson said.

"Hey," the girl sitting next to him said to get his attention. "What's your name?"

"Didn't you just hear him tell Mr. Johnson his name, gurl?" a nappy-headed boy said.

The girl turned around and shot him a nasty glare. She didn't say a word, just looked at him. He tried to stare her down but couldn't and turned away. She kept staring until he placed his head on his desk.

"Franky," he said. "What's yours?"

"It's Khadija," she said with a pretty smile that showed off the straightest and whitest teeth Franky had ever seen. "You got a girlfriend?"

"Nope," he said. "Why do you ask?"

"I'm just asking, but I think you're lying. You're too fine not to have one," she said.

Franky stopped writing and looked at her. He hadn't really paid her too much attention before, but now that she was trying to push up on him, he really studied her.

She was cute, and she would be even cuter if she took all that colorful yarn out of her hair. Khadija's skin was a deep mocha and was as smooth as a baby's bottom. Her eyes were a little big for her small face, yet they sparkled with life. Franky looked down at her thighs, which were nice and thick in her tight jeans. He wondered if she ran track or played any sports. She had on a pair of high-top sneakers with colors that matched her polo shirt and hair.

Khadija kept chewing her gum and blowing bubbles while she watched him watching her.

"Thank you. Are you gonna take any notes?" he asked, finally turning away from her.

"Nope," she said. "I already know this stuff."

"Oh, yeah," he said. "Maybe you can help me catch up. I haven't been to school in a minute."

"Maybe I can, maybe I can't," she said. "I don't know. We'll have to see."

"Do you have a boyfriend?" Franky asked while he wrote.

"No," she said quickly. "I don't have time for these lames around here. Most of these dudes at this school can't handle a girl like me."

"A girl like you? And what type of girl are you?" Franky asked.

"A real one. And only real dudes can recognize and appreciate a chick like me," she said. "Where are you from? You sound funny."

Franky laughed and shook his head. "I'm from New Orleans," he said. "And you sound funny to me. Where are you from?"

"ATL, shawty. Yep. Born and raised right here. I'm a Grady baby," she said before blowing another bubble.

"What's a Grady baby?" he asked.

"That's the hospital where I was born. Grady Memorial. Get it, Grady baby?" she said.

"I got it."

"It was a fool from New Orleans who shot my potna," a voice said directly behind Franky.

"It wasn't me," Franky said, not even bothering to turn around.

"How I know that? You put in the mind of one of 'em, so I might just take my frustrations out on you. Even if it wasn't you," the boy said.

Stand tall. Send a message. Don't let nobody punk you.

Franky stopped writing and turned around to face the boy who seemed to be looking for trouble. Other than the time he took a trip to Africa with his parents, he had never seen skin as dark as this guy's. He was almost the color of coal and had bloodshot eyes. His hair was short and nappy, but he had slanted eyes as if his ancestors were of Asian descent.

"Why would you do that? I never even shot anybody. I don't even own a gun," Franky said.

"You might wanna get one, homeboi," the boy said, then stood up and walked out of the classroom without even asking for a hall pass.

Franky turned to Khadija and frowned as if to ask her what that was all about.

"That's Tyrone. He's a thug—or at least he wants to be one. Don't worry about him. He just likes attention," Khadija said. "Just punch him in the eye one good time and he'll leave you alone."

Franky sighed and shook his head.

"So you want my number or what?" Khadija asked.

"Of course," he said with a smile. "You seem like you're

good people. Besides, you gotta help me catch up on this work in here."

"I am cool, and we'll see about the help," she said, blowing another bubble. "What's your cell number?"

"I don't have a cell phone," he said.

"What?" she asked as if he had just said he didn't have a head on his shoulders.

"I don't have one. Is that a crime?"

"Well, when you get one, I'll give you my number. Is that fair enough?" she asked.

"Nope, but it's your number, so what can I do? And you should still take notes even if you know this stuff already."

"Why?"

"Because what else do you have to do?"

"Text my friends," she said.

"You can do that at home," he said.

"Okay, Dad," she said, closing her phone and pulling out a tablet from her book bag. "See. You're already a good influence on me. I like that."

Franky laughed and tore off his first page of notes and handed it to her. "I'll help you even if you don't want to help me," he said.

"I never said I wasn't going to," Khadija said. She wrote her number down on a piece of paper and handed it to Franky. "You better be glad I love that accent. I wanna hear it again tonight around eight."

"Fo sho," Franky said, and slipped the number into his pocket.

8

Franky walked out of the school building among the sea of teenagers who seemed to be happy that their day had finally come to an end. For the first time in almost three years, he felt right. The school itself wasn't what he was used to, but that was okay; he would adapt. He was good at adapting and was sure he'd get used to the place the kids called M&M High. He walked down the steps and took in the scenery of the high school campus. He was in dire need of a book bag because his teachers loaded him down with four thick textbooks and a not-so-thick one for his technology class. He saw a few familiar faces from his neighborhood and nodded at them as he made his way down the school's stairs. He wasn't ready to go home. He had spent too much time in that place since arriving in Atlanta and wasn't in a rush to get back there. He decided he would try to find the football field to see what the team was looking like, but just as he stopped to ask someone where he could find the coach, he heard someone running toward him. He turned around just in time to see the guy who'd tried to start something with him in Mr. Johnson's class.

"Boo," Tyrone said, with a frown on his face.

"What's up?" Franky said casually, turning around to see the blue-black face. He wasn't sure what this guy's deal was, but his antenna went straight up.

"Did I scare ya, boi?"

"No," Franky said. "What can I do for ya?"

"Leave my school. Get from round here. That's what you can do for me, New Orleans," Tyrone said as he stepped so close to Franky that their noses were almost touching.

"You mind backing up out of my face?" Franky said.

"Make me," Tyrone barked, sending saliva into Franky's face as people rushed over to see what was going on.

Stand tall. Don't let nobody punk you. Send a message. Try to break something.

Without a second thought, Franky dropped his books, stepped his right leg back, slightly bent his knee for leverage, and came up with a hard right-hand uppercut to Tyrone's left jaw. The force of the blow caused Tyrone's head to snap back. Franky followed with a quick left cross to the boy's temple, and Tyrone's eyes rolled toward the back of his head. He was unconscious before his body hit the ground. The crowd of onlookers oohed and aahed at the destruction that just took place in a matter of seconds. Franky stepped back with his hands up and his head on a swivel. He was looking for anyone else who might want to join in or come to Tyrone's defense. He wasn't playing the big tough guy; he just didn't want to be blindsided. He heard a loud whistle, and the same two hulking security officers who were manning the metal detector when he first arrived at school came running over to the crowd.

"Back up! Back up!" they yelled. "What happened over here?"

Franky started to say something to defend himself—and likely incriminate himself—but Khadija appeared out of nowhere and looped her arm into his. He pulled away from her, not sure if she was a friend or a foe. Once he saw her smile and realized who she was, he relaxed. She reached down to gather his books for him, and after a few deep breaths, he leaned down to help her. Once they had all of his things, she slipped her arm through his again and led him away from the crowd.

"Oh, nobody seen a thing, huh?" one of the officers asked as he leaned down to check on Tyrone, who was bleeding profusely from the mouth.

"Snitches get stitches," someone yelled from afar.

"Yeah, okay," the officer said. "We're gonna find out who did this once we look at that videotape. But y'all go on and act like ya Ray Charles."

"Looks like he got knocked clean out," the other officer said, trying to stifle a laugh. "Let's get him up."

"Do you walk home or catch the bus?" Khadija asked, her mind no longer on the fight that just took place. It was a daily occurrence at M&M High.

"I'm walking," Franky said, still amped about the fight that took him totally by surprise. "I'm going to get suspended on my first day of school. What's that dude's problem?"

"No, you won't get suspended," she said. "Nobody's gonna tell those rent-a-cops anything. They couldn't get directions if they were lost."

"But what about the videotape?" Franky asked.

"What about it?"

"They're gonna see me on the tape," he said, wondering how his parents would feel about the way he handled the situation. His dad would've been proud and given him a high five; his mother would've been appalled and chastised him for not walking away.

"Those lazy bustas ain't looking at no tape. Especially about no measly little fight. Stop yo worrying, shawty. You're good."

"Man," he said, "all I wanted to do was come to school. Why did that guy try to start something with me? I don't know him, and he doesn't know me."

"I told you he likes attention," she said, looking back at the officers, who had Tyrone sitting now. They were waving some smelling salts back and forth under his nose. "He's getting all the attention he can stand now. That's what he gets tryna jump bad."

"Yeah. I guess you're right," Franky said, looking over at his victim.

"You won't have no more problems out of him," Khadija said proudly. "Trust me on that."

"I hope not," Franky said. "I don't like fighting, ya heard."

"Yeah, I hear ya. But you're oh so good at it, shawty," Khadija said with a wink.

"Stop calling me shorty. I'm taller than you," he said, slowly coming down from the high of his altercation.

"Yeah, but you're still my shawty," Khadija said, and rubbed his arm.

"Whatever you say, Mrs. Blue and Red Hair," he said.

"Don't hate," she said.

"Well, I do hate it," Franky said.

"For real?"

"For real. You're too pretty to have all of that mess in your hair looking like an ice-cream swirly."

"Oh, you got jokes?"

"I'm just saying."

"So you think I'm pretty?"

"Yeah," he said with a smile. "You're pretty."

"Why you got all these books, man? They didn't give you a locker?"

"Yeah, but I told you I need to play catch-up," he said, shifting the books to his other hand.

"Okay. If you say so, shawty," she said. "Have at it."

Franky smiled and peeked over his shoulder to see if the officers were looking at him. They weren't. They were busy trying to get Tyrone to stand on his own.

"Okay, Franky. I gotta get on this bus before I get left. Then I'll have to call my momma, and Lord knows I don't wanna hear her mouth. But you make sure you call me tonight. Okay?"

"Fo sho," he said as he watched her run off to where a line of cheese buses waited.

If she takes that crap out of her hair, we might be working with something, he thought.

9

After his altercation with Tyrone, Franky walked around
the building to check on the football team. He walked
around the building to check out the football team. He
stood at the fence and watched the M&M Rams practice
for about twenty minutes or so. They seemed to be pretty
good. He could tell the coach had their full attention. It
was totally different from what he saw in the classrooms.
He made a mental note to speak with the coach tomorrow
to see if he could get out there and in the mix. It had been
so long since he had participated in football that he wasn't
sure if he was fast enough to handle playing tailback anymore. He had had a nice little growth spurt in the last few
years. He showed up in Atlanta as a skinny, five-feet-two-
inch twelve-year-old but was now a five-feet-ten-inch fifteen-
year-old who weighed close to one hundred and seventy
pounds. Maybe he would try linebacker, or maybe he
would just tell the coach to pick a spot for him. Standing
there watching his peers, he realized how much he missed

football. Just watching was starting to torture him, so he stepped back from the fence and headed home. He took the scenic route even though those heavy books were starting to give his arms fits. He passed Morehouse College and Clark Atlanta University and was hopeful that he would one day join the kids he saw milling about the huge campus.

As soon as he turned onto his street, he saw his friend Jason sitting on the front steps of his house. There was something about the way he was sitting—hands wrapped around his knees with his head down—that made Franky walk over to him.

"What's wrong with you, whoadie?" he said as he approached his little friend.

"I'm locked out and Grandma ain't answering the door," Jason said, seemingly on the verge of tears. "I been out here forever, and I gotta go to the bathroom and do the number two."

Franky walked past him and up the steps to the house. He knocked on the door as hard as he could, but there was no answer.

"Well, come on over to our house and use the bathroom," Franky said. "Do you have anyone you can call?"

"Yeah," Jason said. "My auntie Samantha or my cousin David but their numbers is in the house."

"*Are*," Franky said, correcting Jason the way his mother used to correct him. "Their numbers *are* in the house. Come on."

"Whatchu doing with books?" Jason asked.

"I just got home from school," he said proudly. "What do you think I'm doing with 'em?"

"You in school now?" Jason asked as he walked beside Franky.

"Yep."

"No more dummy for you," Jason said, but Franky could see that his mind was clearly on his grandmother.

Franky was worried about Mrs. Bertha, too. In all the time they had lived across the street from her, she had never missed a day of waiting for Jason. Something wasn't right. She would normally be sitting in her rocking chair, waiting on his bus to arrive.

They walked across the street to Franky's house. When they walked in, Franky noticed Rico spread out on the sofa fast asleep. An empty beer bottle was on the floor, and he wore only a pair of boxer shorts.

"Go ahead. You know where the bathroom is," Franky said as he looked down at his cousin with new disdain. He loved Rico, but he didn't like him. And Rico's little charade this morning didn't do anything to help with his feelings toward his cousin. He walked into his bedroom, and his anger grew even more. Clothes were everywhere. Worse than it was this morning before he left for school. He placed his books on his dresser and looked at the mess of clothes. He took a deep breath and started picking up his things. He neatly folded every piece of clothing, then placed them in his closet. Once he was halfway through with his task, he heard the toilet flush and Jason walked out.

"Y'all nasty," Jason said with his face frowned up. "Somebody didn't even flush the toilet. My grandmother would hit y'all with her broom. And why y'all toilet paper so hard?"

"Man," Franky said, throwing a pair of socks at Jason. "Shut up."

"Why yo room so messy?"

"Why do you talk so much?" Franky said.

"What dat got to do with anything?"

"Boy, be quiet," Franky said. "What are you gonna do about getting in touch with your family, lil whoadie?"

"I don't know. I used to be able to crawl through the window until Grandma put bars on them. Where my grandma at?"

"How am I supposed to know? I just got home from school."

"Oh," Jason said, tears welling up in his eyes. "She might be in the house sick. Or even dead."

"Nah," Franky said. "She's okay. I just saw her this morning. She helped me get in school."

Jason seemed to relax a little. "How she get there?" he asked.

Before Franky could respond, he heard the house phone ring and rushed into the kitchen to get it.

"Hello?" Franky said.

There was a four-second pause.

"Hello?" he said again.

"This is a call from an inmate at the Atlanta City Detention Center," the automated voice said; then he heard his cousin's voice say, "Nigel." The automatic voice kicked in again. "Will you accept charges?"

"Yes," Franky said.

"Do not use call forwarding or three-way calling or your call will be disconnected," the recording said, then clicked and Nigel was on the line.

"Yo," Franky said, not really surprised by the call. Since they arrived in Atlanta, Nigel had been arrested two or three times for various infractions, and Rico had been caught up about five or six times.

"Hey, Franky," Nigel said. "How you doing?"

"I'm good," Franky said. "What happened to you?"

"Some mix-up. I need for you to call that lawyer we used the last time and tell her to come holla at me," he said.

"Okay," Franky said, wondering how they were going to come up with money for an attorney when they didn't have any for food.

"Do that as soon as you get off the phone with me, ya heard."

"I will."

"Have you seen Jason?"

"Yeah, he's right here. Mrs. Bertha's not answering the door."

"She's in the hospital. Stick broke into her house. When we got home from taking you to school, I saw the fool running out of the woman's house. She was upset but she seemed a'ight, ya know. But I left to get her stuff back from Stick, and when I got outside, I saw them putting her into the ambulance. That's when the cops jumped out at me. Fools wasn't tryna hear nuttin' I had to say."

"Stick? Why he do that?"

"Because he's Stick. But you can best believe I'ma handle that fool, ya heard? He got me caught up in his mess. I tried doing the right thing and went and got the stuff he stole from her, but the police rolled up on me. You know how those police do us, so it was on. They can't wait to lock a brother up. Get that lawyer on the phone for me. I need to get up outta here, ya heard."

"Yeah, I feel ya," Franky said. "That's messed up."

"Fo sho," Nigel said. "Where is Rico?"

"Sleeping on the sofa," Franky said, rolling his eyes.

"Tell that fool I said get up and go get some money. We

need to grind right now—no time for sleeping. I can't do no time for this one, ya heard. Not for that fool. Yo," Nigel said, as if he just had a thought. "You know what I need? I need for you to run down to Stick's house and tell him I'm locked up because of him. Tell him he owes me and that I'm pissed. You tell that sorry lil piece of trash that I need bail money. But call the lawyer first."

"Okay," Franky said.

"And make Rico go with you so that fool don't act stupid, ya heard."

"Got it," Franky said, but he knew he wasn't going to wake up his volatile cousin. He would let him sleep forever if it was up to him.

"Okay, whoadie," Nigel said. "Handle those things for me and I will call you back in a few hours if I can."

"Okay," Franky said. "I'll get on it right away. Talk to you later."

"Hey, yo," Nigel called out right before Franky took the phone away from his ear.

"Yeah."

"How was school?"

"It was different," Franky said, happy that his cousin asked. "But it was cool. I got in a fight, too."

"A fight?"

"Yeah, this dude ran up on me talking about how some New Orleans guys killed his friend. It wasn't really a fight. I punched him two times and knocked him out," Franky said proudly.

"Okay, Floyd Mayweather," Nigel said with a chuckle. "But don't be up there getting in no trouble. You ain't no street dude, so stay clear of that mess. It'll pull ya down, ya heard."

"Yeah. I met a cool girl, too."

"Ohh, Lord. We'll talk about that one later. Handle that business for me, whoadie," Nigel said.

"I'm on it," Franky said. "Peace."

Franky hung up the phone, opened the kitchen drawer, and searched around for the pad with the number for attorney Sharon Capers. He found it, called the number, and left a message with Nigel's name and the jail where he was located. He knew the drill by now. Once he was done leaving the message, he hung up the phone.

"Listen," Franky said to Jason. "You sit tight for a second. I need to run down the street and holla at somebody."

"Okay," Jason said with a nervous look on his face. He went from being a smart-aleck little boy to a scared one.

"Do you have any homework?" Franky asked.

"Yeah," Jason said.

"Get started on it and I'll be right back."

10

Franky walked down the street and marched up Stick's driveway. The bum was sitting on his front porch in a rocking chair, smoking a cigarette with his feet up on a table.

"What's up witcha, lil buddy?" Stick said to Franky.

"My cousin is pissed off with you."

"Which cousin?"

Franky knew exactly why he was asking that question. Nigel was somewhat of a diplomat and would try his best to work out whatever issue he had with a person by talking. That's why being a drug dealer didn't work out for him; he didn't have or refused to show that killer instinct needed to handle street people. They only responded to fear of violence. Rico, on the other hand, was exactly what the streets needed. And even though they sometimes fought like cats and dog, the brothers had each other's backs.

"Both of them," Franky said. "Nigel is locked up for something you did."

"Locked up?" Stick said, snatching his feet down from the table. "Something I did? Whatchu talking 'bout?"

"That thing that went down at Mrs. Bertha's," Franky said.

Stick was visibly nervous and looked like he was about to jump out of his own skin and run for cover. "Da . . . da . . . that thing was fixed. We straightened that out," he stammered.

"Nope," Franky said, shaking his head and enjoying the bum's discomfort.

"Whatchu mean by that? I mean we talked about that, and I gave him all the stuff back. Wasn't nuttin' to be arrested for," Stick said, seeming on the verge of tears. He was the biggest coward Franky had ever seen, which was why he could always be seen hanging out with people who were half his age.

"Not so. Nigel got caught leaving your house with the stuff. The police arrested him on the spot."

"So that's on him," Stick said. "How is that my fault? I gave him the stuff back. Now, true enough when I found that stuff, I should've taken it right back. 'Cause I didn't break into nobody's house. I found that stuff in the back-yard, and I was gonna take it back when she got home but—"

"Stick," Franky said, cutting off the lie before the bum could really get started. "Rico is pissed. He's talking about doing something real bad to you, but I asked him to let me come talk to you first. You know me and you always been cool."

"Right . . . right . . . right. You a good dude, Franky, and you got a good head on ya shoulders," Stick said as if he sensed an out to his situation.

"So here's what I need. Two things. One for Nigel and the other for me."

"Talk to me," the bum said. "Have a seat. Let's talk bidness."

Franky walked up on the porch and sat in one of the rocking chairs.

"We need bail money," Franky said.

"How much is his bail?"

"Twenty-five thousand dollars."

"What the . . . Twenty-five what?" Stick shouted. "Who in the heck did they say he robbed, Hannah Montana? That's the kind of money they ask for when you rob white folks. Man, I ain't got no twenty-five thousand dollars. If I had that, do you think I would be here? I would be chilling on a tropical island sipping on something fruity and watching me a curvy woman with a straw skirt on."

"Well, you know the bail bondsman asks for only ten percent," Franky said. "Can you do twenty-five hundred?"

"Man, no," Stick said. "I don't have *twenty-five* dollars right now."

"Well, Stick, you're gonna have to do something. Nigel needs to get out. So you can either go down to that jail and turn yourself in or come up with the money. Rico told me I need to have an answer for him in ten minutes. I've been here for about five already. Whatchu gonna do, man?"

Stick rubbed his raggedy beard as he thought about his dilemma.

"What's the other favor you need?"

"Oh," Franky said. "I need for you to break back into

Mrs. Bertha's house. Jason is locked out, and we need to get a telephone number. She's in the hospital, and we need to get in touch with their people."

"Whatchu mean, break back in? I never broke into her house in the first place," Stick said with a straight face.

"Come on, Stick, man," Franky said, standing. "You're wasting time. I gotta get back home."

"Let me think for a minute on the bail situation," he said. "I got a friend who might be able to help you out."

"What about Mrs. Bertha's house?"

Stick jumped to his feet. "Let's go," he said.

Franky and Stick walked down the street together, and once they came up on his house, they saw Rico standing on the porch, still in his underwear.

"Come here, Franky," Rico said.

Franky looked at Stick, whose eyes betrayed him and showed nothing but fear.

"Go ahead and handle that over there," Franky said, pointing at Mrs. Bertha's house.

Stick gladly hurried away from the prying eyes of Rico, who was staring him down. Franky walked over to his cousin.

"Whatchu doing with Stick?" Rico asked.

"Jason is locked out, and I asked Stick to try to open the house so Jason could get in."

"Where's Mrs. Bertha?"

"In the hospital."

"And so why his people didn't come get him?"

"He doesn't know their phone numbers by heart. So that's why we gotta get in the house," Franky said.

"Yo, man," Rico said. "I'm sorry about this morning, ya heard. I was wrong for that."

"Yeah, you were," Franky said. "But it's cool. We're struggling over here, and it's frustrating."

Rico hunched his shoulders as if to say "not really."

"Nigel's locked up," Franky said casually.

Rico frowned. "For what?"

"Burglary. Police think he broke into Mrs. Bertha's."

"Nigel? Nah," Rico said, shaking his head. "That's not his thing. That boy wouldn't burglarize a store even if nobody was in it, and he sure nuff ain't breaking into nobody's house. *I* won't break into nobody's house."

"I know," Franky said, looking over at Mrs. Bertha's house. "Stick did it. Nigel went to get the stuff back from him, and the police showed up. They caught him with the stuff he was trying to return."

"Wait a minute," Rico said. "My brother is locked up behind something that fool did?"

"Yep," Franky said.

"And how do you know all this when you were supposed to be at school?"

"He just called when I got home. You were asleep."

"Oh, okay. Gotcha," Rico said, nodding at Stick, who was walking around the side of Mrs. Bertha's house. "So what that fool gonna do?"

"Nigel told me to get the bail money from him," Franky said. "But of course he's claiming he doesn't have it. He said he will check with his people."

"His people? Yeah, okay. He better do something or I will," Rico said, staring at the bum who was now his enemy.

"Did you get in?" he said, turning to Stick.

"Yep," Stick said proudly. He gave a thumbs-up and started toward his house. It was clear he wanted to avoid Rico at all costs. "The back door is open."

"Cool," Franky said, and walked past his cousin and into their house.

"Come here, man," Rico said to Stick. "We need to talk."

Stick shook his head and took off running down the street. He looked like a big goofy chicken as he ran while looking back over his shoulder.

Rico chuckled and didn't bother to give chase.

11

Franky sat on the steps of his house with Jason. Neither one of the boys said much; both were lost in their own thoughts. They were waiting on one of Jason's relatives to show up.

"Jason," Franky said, breaking the silence and throwing his arm around Jason's little shoulder. "You're going to be okay, lil whoadie."

"But when is my grandma coming home?"

"I don't know, but we all know she's a strong woman, and she's gonna beat whatever this is that messing with her," Franky said.

"She don't have muscles. It's just fat," Jason said with his head down.

"Not that kind of strong, boy," Franky said, shaking his head. "She's strong in the brain, and when you believe something hard enough, a lot of times it helps your body make it happen. As bad as you are, she's crazy about you, so you know she's gonna fight extra hard."

"I'm not bad," Jason said.

"Well, what do you call it, Jason? Because where I'm from, we call it bad with a capital *B*."

"My teacher said you shouldn't call kids bad because they will start acting like that. She told me I'm a good boy," Jason said, rolling his eyes and bouncing his head from side to side. "Now what you got to say to that, Mr. I'm Fifteen and I Already Quit School?"

"I didn't quit school, chump. Didn't you just see me with a bunch of books?"

"You probably stole them from somebody."

"I don't steal. And your teacher is crazy. You're bad. Super bad. You're probably the baddest little boy I've ever seen in my life. You have supernatural powers that make you extra bad, whoadie."

"Nuh-uh," Jason said. "My grandma told me that I'm her angel."

Franky chuckled. "You know what, Jason? Your grandmother and your teachers are right. You do bad things, but you're not a bad kid. You just do stuff to get attention, but it's the wrong kind of attention. I checked your homework, and you got all of the answers right. Everybody knows you're smart, so why not use it and stop trying to get on people's nerves?"

"How you know what everybody knows? You ever talk to everybody? Have you talked to all the people in China, Asia, Mars?"

"Mars?"

"Martians," Jason said, twisting his lip up. "You so dumb."

"Call me dumb again and I'm going to smack you right upside your lil knotty head," Franky said.

"Okay," Jason said, then scratched his head. "What about stupid?"

"Shut up," Franky said. "Like I was saying. You're smart enough to know that you shouldn't be doing some of the stuff you do."

"Stuff like what?"

"Stealing, fighting, talking back to your grandmother, sneaking out of the house. Should I continue? You're only seven years old. Why would you sneak out of the house? What if somebody kidnaps you? Whatchu gonna do then?"

"I wish a fool would try to kidnap me. I'll kick him in the nuts and bite him. I bet he won't try to kidnap nobody else. I ain't scared of no kidnapper."

Franky laughed. "Yeah, they'll probably bring your lil bad butt back."

"They better," Jason said. "I'm staying with my grandma not some crazy kidnapper."

"Where is your mother and father, Jason?" Franky asked, even though he already knew that Jason's father had always been a no-show and his mother was living her life with a rich man across town. The man didn't want kids, so Jason was pawned off on Mrs. Bertha. With the exception of the day he was born, Jason had never met the woman.

"My momma lives in California," he said proudly. "She's rich. She makes movies."

"Is that right?"

"Yeah, she said she's gonna come get me when she finishes working. And when I get out to California, I'ma make me a rap record with Snoop Dogg."

"Can you rap?" Franky asked.

"Yeah, stupid," Jason said.

"That's it," Franky said, grabbing the little boy and play-fully putting him in a headlock.

"You said dumb . . . you said dumb," Jason said through his laughter as he tried to cover up. "You said I couldn't call you dumb. Not stupid, stupid."

A car pulled up across the street at Mrs. Bertha's house, and a lady got out and walked up to the house. Jason stood up and sighed. Franky could tell he didn't want to go.

"I guess that's your ride, lil whoadie," Franky said, re-leasing him.

"Yeah. That's my aunt. She's mean. I wish I could just stay over here with y'all until my grandma gets out of the hospital," he said.

"Nah," Franky said. "You need to take your lil butt with your aunt. I gave you our telephone number, so if you need me, just call, okay?"

"Okay," Jason said reluctantly. "But I really need to stay with y'all, because who's gonna help you with your home-work?"

"I think I'll manage," Franky said as he rubbed Jason's head. They stood and walked across the street. Jason's aunt didn't even bother to look his way. She didn't say thank you for watching her nephew or even a quick hello.

Jason walked over to the passenger side and paused. He waved to Franky and wore a look that was so sad Franky felt sorry for him. Franky waved back and hoped that he would see his little buddy again soon.

12

Franky sat at the kitchen table going over his textbooks. He was surprised at how quickly he picked up the work. He took a few of the practice tests, which were at the end of each chapter and scored in the low eighties. Not bad for someone who hadn't seen the inside of a classroom in years.

He looked at the clock on the wall in the kitchen. It was almost nine o'clock. He was hoping that Nigel would come walking through the door, but the house was totally quiet. Rico had gone out as usual, and for the first time in a long while, Franky got some much-needed peace and quiet. He walked over and grabbed the cordless telephone off the counter. He stuck his hand in his back pocket and came out with Khadija's telephone number. He stared at the girl's handwriting and how she put a little heart at the bottom of her name. Was that normal or was that for him? He dialed the number and she picked up.

"Hello?" Khadija said.

"What's up?" Franky said. "This is Franky, from school."

"New Orleans," she said, her joy jumping through the phone. "I see you're still on that central time. I said eight o'clock, boy."

"Why are you fussing already?" Franky asked.

"Because I hate when people don't follow directions," Khadija said.

"I had a lot going on when I got home, so I apologize. If it's too late, I can talk to you at school tomorrow."

"Boy, stop," she said. "You're straight. Actually, I just got in the house, too. My dad just came home from Iraq today. So I've been hanging with him getting spoiled."

Franky zeroed in on how different she sounded. At school there was a hardness, but on the phone she sounded like a typical suburban girl.

"What did you do today after school, besides fight?" she said with a giggle.

"Don't even remind me of that one."

"I'm glad you did that. Now you won't have to worry about nobody around there running their mouth any-more. Trust me—the word is already around the school. My phone's been blowing up since I got home. Every-body's asking me about you. They talking about 'What's up with yo boyfriend? I heard he knocked Tyrone out.' I told them you're not my boyfriend."

"Why did you have to say it like that?" he asked with a chuckle. "You act like something is wrong with me. Do I have an extra hand growing out of my forehead or some-thing?"

"Oh, hush, shawty. It ain't like that. I'm just saying. We just met. Like I said, I gotta check you out first. See if you're worthy of the princess."

"Princess, huh?" Franky said.

"That's right. My daddy is the king, my mother is the queen, so what does that make me?"

"I guess that makes you the princess."

"That's right. And I need a prince, not a clown. I don't do thugs. They are disgusting."

"Well, don't put me in the thug category. What happened after school was on him. I don't bother anybody. I'm not that kind of guy."

"What kind of guy are you talking about? You were defending yourself," she said. "It's not like you went looking for trouble. He did and I'm glad he found it with his ugly self."

"Not really. He didn't hit me. I could've walked away."

"Whatever. I wouldn't worry about it. Are you a quiet guy, Franky?"

"I am if I don't have anything to say."

"Don't get smart, shawty. You know what I mean."

"I'm just saying. I'm not really a loudmouth if that's what you're asking, but I'm not afraid to talk."

"When did you move here from New Orleans?"

"Right after Hurricane Katrina."

"So where did you go to school before you came to M and M?"

"I went to school in New Orleans."

"But you said you came here after Katrina."

"I did."

"Wait a minute. Hurricane Katrina was years ago."

"I know. Trust me. I know exactly when it was."

Franky took a deep breath, and even though he never shared his story with strangers, he decided to share with her. He went through all of the details of the storm, his father and his uncle dying because neither one of them could leave his grandmother to die in a house that she refused to leave. He shared with her how his mother's parents never wanted anything to do with him or her since she married outside of her race. He told her about how he and his cousins stayed in the dome for a little over a week with very little food or any real help from the government. Finally he told her about the trip to Atlanta where he and his cousins had been fending for themselves for almost three years now.

"Wow," she said. "Oh my God, Franky. I'm so sorry to hear that. Wow. I don't know what to say."

"It's all right. I'm getting back into the swing of things. Slowly but surely," Franky said.

"I'm stunned," Khadija said. "I'm sitting over here crying my eyes out."

"Don't do that," he said. "It's life. Lots of families were ruined because of Katrina."

"I know, but I didn't know anybody down there, so to me it was something I saw on TV, but now . . ." she said. "Man. I don't know what to say. That's crazy. I wouldn't know what to do without my mom and dad."

"Yeah, that's the toughest part," Franky said. "I don't know if I'll ever get over losing them."

"I knew there was something special about you."

"There is nothing special about me. I just went through the storms like everybody else. I survived, but sometimes I wish I would've died with my dad," Franky said.

"Franky," she said. "Don't say that. God left you here for a reason."

"Oh, yeah," he said. "What reason could that be? To suffer? Because that's all I've been doing."

"No," she said, showing a sign of maturity that she didn't at school. "Your story hasn't been written yet. My dad says that being a teenager is your foundation years. You build a bad one and your whole adult life will come crumbling down."

"Your dad sounds like my dad," Franky said.

"Maybe all dads sound the same," she said. "If they are about anything. Now I see why you were up in class doing your work so hard. That's that private school still in ya."

"I guess. I missed school, and I really need to find me a book bag."

"Yeah. Especially if you're gonna be taking your books home every night."

"I need to bring them home so I can catch up. I'm lost up in there."

"I understand," she said. "I'll bring you a book bag to school tomorrow. I have plenty of them from basketball and stuff."

"Thanks. But now you know all there is to know about me, so it's your turn. Tell me about you," Franky said.

"Well, let's see," Khadija started. "I'm the youngest of three kids. My oldest sister is in college at the University of Washington in Seattle. I don't know why she wanted to go all the way out there, but she seems to like it, so who am I to complain? My older brother is . . . well . . . Let's just say he's trying to find himself, and the state of Georgia's judicial system is giving him a nice little place to stay while he does it."

"So he's locked up," Franky said.

"Ding, ding, ding," she said. "You are correct. And it's a shame, too, because he's so nice, but he wants to be a gangster. Why I do not know."

"I see. Although it's nice to hear about your sister and brother, I want to know about the girl who wears the blue and red stuff in her hair."

"You really don't like my hair like this, do you?"

"Nope," he said. "It looks crazy. Royal-blue and fire-engine-red yarn? That's too much going on."

"Okayyyyyy," she whined. "I'll take it out tonight."

"You don't have to do that for me. It's your hair."

"I know that. Maybe I'll leave it in since you don't care one way or the other," she said.

"Will you please get back to telling me about you?" he said.

"I'm simple. Not much to me. I run track and play basketball for M and M. Oh, and I'm in the SAE. But overall I live a pretty boring life. I spend my free time on Facebook and Twitter. Do you tweet?"

"What?"

"I guess that answers my question."

"What is SAE?"

"Student Action for Education," she said proudly.

"How are you in the Student Action for Education when you don't even do your schoolwork?"

"I do my work, shawty," Khadija said. "I don't know what you're talking about. I've never had anything less than a B in my life, shawty. And I had only one of those. I told you I know that stuff Mr. Johnson was writing already. I took Spanish in middle school, plus I got Rosetta Stone."

"Is that right? Well, I apologize."

"No need for all that. Just know that I'm on it doggone it," Khadija said. "I like when people underestimate me. They do that on the basketball court, too. The girls are saying I'm not gonna make the varsity as a freshman. I'm like, we'll see. Not only am I gonna make it, but I'ma start, too. They don't want me to come out there because they know somebody's spots getting got."

"Listen to you," Franky said. "Ms. Confidence. I guess you're pretty good, huh?"

"I'm straight," she said.

"I went to look at the football team practice after school. They look pretty good. I'ma go talk to the coach tomorrow."

"Oh, yeah. That's good. Why aren't you in my other classes?"

"One of my friends told me that I'm in the dumb classes," he said with a frown. "The lady in the front office told me they placed me there because they didn't have my school records from my old school and because it's been a while since I've attended, so they'll have to see."

"Yeah," she said. "That's understandable. Hopefully they'll move you soon. You gotta role with the gifted. 'The nerds' as they like to call us."

"I don't know when I'm taking that test, but I hope they hurry up and give it to me," he said. "Hold on for a minute."

Franky heard some commotion outside of his house and jumped up to see what was going on. He ran to the front door and saw Rico on top of Stick. He was pummeling him senseless, and Stick was pleading for his life like the scared coward he was. Franky ran back to the phone.

"Khadija," he said, his voice rising. "I'll see you tomorrow at school. My cousin is outside fighting."

"Okay," she said. "You can call me back later if you want. I'll be up late."

"Okay," Franky said, and hung up the phone.

He rushed outside to see if he could get his cousin to stop. There was a crowd of at least twenty people, and it seemed that Stick had done all of them wrong at least once, because no one made a move to help the old bum. Just as Franky was stepping off the last step, he heard a huge explosion. It was a gunshot. Rico looked up as the crowd scattered every which way. Rico stopped hitting Stick and stared into the eyes of Stick's mother. She had the gun pointed at him.

"You better take your hands off of my boy or it'll be the last time you take a breath," the surprisingly young-looking woman said.

Rico still had Stick by his collar with his fist balled up in the ready position. He looked like he was about to punch him again, but then he paused and looked to his right.

"Rico!" Franky yelled, stopping his cousin from what seemed to be a premature death.

Rico took a few deep breaths and turned away. He looked back at the neighborhood bum, who had dirt and leaves all in his hair and a bloody nose. "You better fix this situation with my brother, or I promise you the next time I won't stop, ya heard."

"I ain't gonna ask you twice to get your filthy hands off of my baby," Stick's mother said.

Rico pushed the skinny man down onto the ground and stood up. He stared at the woman as if daring her to shoot him.

"You have a good night," he said, and kicked Stick in his ribs before walking over him and toward his house.

"You got a death wish, boy," Stick's mother said before rushing over to help her sorry son to his feet.

Franky followed Rico into the house and paused as his cousin paced back and forth to let off a little steam.

"We gotta get Nigel out," he said. "I don't mind him sitting in there if he got caught doing his dirt, but I'll be a snake in the grass if he do one day behind the fence for that fool, Stick. He at home chillin' and my brother in there doing his time. That just can't happen. Nah, I won't be able to sleep. And that trash he got for a momma gonna regret the day she pulled a gun on me. You pull a gun on me, you better use it."

Franky listened to his cousin rant and knew there was truth to everything that he said. He didn't like Stick nor did he care too much for the woman who enabled him, but he didn't wish them any harm.

"Do you know if Nigel paid that rent?"

"Yeah. He paid it. He dropped it off with the landlord before he took me to school," Franky said.

"Dag," he snapped. "I needed that money. I gotta get some dough, whoadie. I'm going a different route than that lawyer. I wish they would just let Mrs. Bertha have a visitor, and she can fix this whole mess—that is, if they cops go holla at her."

"What you mean you going a different route?"

"Don't worry 'bout it, whoadie. I just need to get my hands on some cash."

"I know a dude who might be able to let me hold something. I'ma have to pay him back, though," Franky said, thinking of the money that was stuffed in his brush.

Rico looked at him as if he knew something wasn't right. Franky was probably the world's worst liar, but the streets had taught him that he'd better get good at it if he was going to survive.

"Get what you can and I'll make sure he gets it back,"
Rico said.

"I'll see him at school tomorrow."

"Good. Get that because what I got in mind ain't cheap,
but it's gonna work."

13

The school was buzzing about the new boy and how he knocked out bigmouthed Tyrone. Everywhere Franky went, people spoke to him, nodded at him, pointed at him, and some of the kids even walked up and shook his hand. He was confused by his newfound popularity and didn't like it one bit. He was standing in the hallway fiddling around with his locker when Khadija walked up.

"Here ya go," she said, handing him a book bag.

"Thanks, Khadija," he said.

"I thought you were gonna call me back last night."

"How are you gonna be a princess if you don't know how to speak to folks?" he asked.

"Hello, Franky. How are you doing this fine morning at M and M High?"

"I'm good. How are you?"

"Just dandy. Now stop dodging my question: Why didn't you call me back last night?"

"I'm sorry about that. Things got crazy after I got off the phone with you. My cousin Rico beat this dude up, and the dude's mom pulled a gun out and started shooting. Then the police came out and started asking questions, but of course nobody told them anything. It was just a bunch of drama," Franky said as he finally got his locker open. He shoved his books inside and kept the two for his next classes.

"Is your cousin okay?" Khadija asked.

"Yeah," he said. "He's okay. I'm a little worried about my oldest cousin, Nigel, though. He's still locked up, and he didn't call like he said he would."

"Maybe he will call you today when you get home," she said.

"I hope so," Franky said.

He looked at her hair and nodded his head approvingly at the braids without the colorful yarn. "Nice. Now you look like a human being. Maybe even a princess."

"Whateva, shawty. What did I look like before?"

"A nut," he said.

She reached over and punched him on the shoulder.

"Ouch," Franky said. "Girl, you hit hard. Are you sure you're a female? I know this is Atlanta, but I don't do that same-sex stuff."

"You wanna get knocked out?" she said, drawing back her little fist.

"No, ma'am—or sir," Franky said, and braced himself for another punch.

The bell rang, and it was time for them to go to their classes.

"A'ight, dude. I'll see you in Spanish class," Khadija said. "Try not to get into any fights until I see you, okay?"

"I'll try," he said, and walked off toward his English class.

Right before Franky walked into his class, he heard his name being called. He turned around to see Bubba waving him over. He walked to where Bubba and Nard were standing.

"What's up?" he said, shaking both of their hands.

"You killing that polo shirt," Nard said. "I like the big horse ones. Where you get that from?"

"I don't know, whoadie," Franky said. "My cousin Rico gave it to me. He comes up with all kinds of things all the time. I'll see if he can look out for ya."

"Oh, yeah. Franky always rocking them freshest gear," Bubba said.

"Man, I'ma holla at y'all later. I need to get to this class. I was registering yesterday round this time, so this will be my first day in here. Gotta make a good impression, ya know."

"Yeah," Bubba said. "I feel ya. But listen, we wanted to see if you was interested in making a lil extra money."

"How?" Franky asked eagerly. All he could think about was getting his cousin out of jail.

"We'll talk about it after school," Bubba said.

"A'ight," Franky said before shaking their hands again and walking off.

"Hold up, Franky," Nard said. "I got this class, too. How you like the school so far?"

"It's cool," Franky said, noticing how nice Nard had all of a sudden become. Just yesterday he was mean-mugging him.

"I heard you knocked Tyrone out cold," Nard said.

Franky grunted. Now he saw the reason for the sudden

change of heart. It was amazing the guys who frowned at you before they knew you could knock that frown upside down. He guessed Nard was in that crowd and figured it'd be better to be friends than enemies.

"It was nothing, man," Franky said, and walked into the class.

English class should've been called the zoo. Ms. Chappell, a twenty-two-year-old white woman who had just graduated from college, had no business teaching at an inner-city school. She stood before the class seemingly on the verge of tears as the kids made more noise than a group of two-year-olds. Nard walked in and started teasing her about her clothes. Franky didn't see anything wrong with what the teacher had on, but that didn't stop the fat boy from giving her the business.

"Whatchu do, get dressed in the dark?" Nard said. "And where you get that Orphan Annie shirt from? You look a hot mess."

"If you insist on being disrespectful, I'm going to write you up," she said without much conviction.

"Shut the hell up," someone said.

"Is this what you guys come to school for? To get a laugh?" Ms. Chappell said. "To talk about people? And you wonder why you can't find a job?"

"Who can't find a job? Do you mean black people?" a girl asked, standing up and rolling her neck. "You a racist and I don't want you to be my teacher no more."

"I'm not a racist," Ms. Chappell said, and seemed genuinely offended. "Why would I choose to work in a school that's almost one hundred percent African American if I was a racist?"

" 'Cause you stupid," the same girl said. "I'm outta here."

"Tanisha, sit down," Ms. Chappell said, but to no avail.

"Nah," Tanisha said, walking out of the class. "I don't like racist white people. I got a bad temper, and I just saw *Roots*. Fuse real short right about now, so it's best I leave this classroom before somebody gets hurt."

"She ain't mad—she just want an excuse to get out of class," Antonio, the short snoring kid from Franky's Spanish class, said.

Tanisha turned around and gave him a laugh before walking out of the door.

Ms. Chappell huffed and walked back to her desk. She stood there staring at the class, shaking her head.

Franky walked over and sat at a desk in the front row. He looked at the teacher, who already seemed defeated. He felt sorry for her. He was embarrassed by the way his peers were carrying on. They were acting like animals, and he hated them for it.

"Hey, yo, Ms. Chappell," Nard said. "Can I go to the bathroom?"

"No, you cannot go to the bathroom," she snapped. "Every single day that you come in here, you ask to go to the bathroom. School has just started, and you should've used the bathroom at home or before you came to class. Now sit down and take out your textbook."

"Who you talking to?" Nard said.

"I'm talking to you, Bernard," she said, marching around her desk as if she had finally snapped and was ready for war. "I've tried my best to be nice to you people."

"Whoa," almost the entire class said at once.

"What do you mean, 'you people'?" a kid asked.

"She means black people," another student said.

"You people as in young people in this class," Ms.

Chappell said, trying to clean up her statement. "You guys seem to think life is one big joke. Do you really think it's funny to come to school and throw away an education? The sad part about it is you guys are only setting yourself up for a bleak future. What kind of life do you expect to have without an education?"

"Shut up," Nard said.

"Is that the best you can come up with, Bernard? When you don't have anything intelligent to say, your response is 'shut up'?"

"Yep. Since I don't have no kind of education, that's 'bout the best I can do," Nard said, much to the delight of the classroom.

Franky stood and walked over to the teacher. He handed her his schedule.

"Nice to meet you, Franklin," she said.

"It's Franky, and it's nice to meet you, too."

"I apologize that your first day has to be like this."

"It's no big deal," Franky said, hunching his shoulders. "I know I missed three weeks of school already, and I was wondering if I could get the makeup work."

"Absolutely," she said, almost too enthusiastic.

The class was so loud that he could barely hear the lady, and she was standing less than two feet away from him. They were getting on his nerves, but he didn't say anything. He walked back to his desk and took a seat.

"Take your books out and turn to page twenty-seven," Ms. Chappell said. "We will start where we left off yesterday."

Franky looked around and didn't see one person pull out their book. Nard stood up and walked out.

"Bernard," Ms. Chappell called out to him, but all he did was fan her off and kept walking.

"Ms. Chappell," Franky said, waving his hand to get her attention.

She turned to him but didn't answer. She wore her frustration all over her face, and the kids took full advantage of it.

"May I go talk to him?" he said, nodding toward the door that Nard had just walked out of.

Ms. Chappell nodded, and Franky jumped up and headed out of the classroom.

"Nard," Franky called out once he was in the hallway.

"What's up, playboi?" he said, stopping to allow Franky to catch up.

"Why are you giving that lady such a hard time, man?"

"I don't know," Nard said, smiling. "Ain't got nuttin' else to do."

Franky sighed. "That's not cool, man."

"Why it ain't?"

"What's up with the money y'all talking about making?" Franky asked, getting to the real reason he wanted to leave the classroom.

"You down?" Nard asked.

"Depends on what y'all talking about."

"Well, my man got some stuff. This stuff will pretty much sell itself. I'll share more details with ya once I know you're in. We see that you be fresh and figured you might have a few extra dollars to make some more. Just wanted to know if you wanted to be down."

"What's it gonna cost me?"

"Depends on what you wanna do."

"Meaning?" Franky asked.

"Well, it means if you invest a lil money, your cut is one thing, but if you wanna get a little deeper, then it's another. Still decent money no matter which way you go."

"How much are you guys talking about?" Franky asked, knowing full well that he wouldn't be selling any kind of drugs.

"You give me two hundred and I'll get you five hundred by Friday. You get me four hundred and I'll get you a thousand bucks by Friday and so on."

"So it's that simple, huh?"

"Pretty much. So whatchu gonna do, barbecue or mildew?"

"A'ight," Franky said, feeling himself crossing over into a world he always said he didn't want any part of. "Come holla at me after school, but I never wanna know what you guys are doing. I don't care. I just need to make some money."

"Sounds good to me," Nard said, walking away. "See no evil, hear no evil."

"And, Nard," he called out.

"What?"

"Come back to class and give the lady a break. We are in there acting like we belong in a zoo."

"Most of them fools do belong in a zoo."

"Maybe, but those same people respect you, man. So I bet if you act right, then they will, too."

"What?" Nard asked with a confused look on his face. "Why do you care about what that skinny lil white girl thinks about us?"

"It's not about her. Even though she shouldn't be talked to like that," Franky said, walking away. "Are you coming?"

Nard looked at Franky like he was from another planet. Franky turned around and walked backward, keeping his eyes on Nard. Nard dropped his head and shook it. "I can't believe I'm letting you talk me into going back to that bony lil white chick's class."

"Aww, come on," Franky said, slapping his arm around Nard's neck once he caught up to him. "It'll be good for you to do the right thing every now and then."

"I'll go back, but I ain't doing jack," Nard said. "So don't ask me to."

Franky laughed and held the door for him to enter.

14

"**G**randma," Jason said through sniffles. "She . . . she . . . she's dead."

Franky held the phone up to his ear in a state of shock. His little friend was crying so hard he could hardly make out what he was saying.

"Jason," Franky said, trying to get a word in between the little boy's sobbing. "Calm down a little bit, whoadie."

"She dead. She told me she wasn't ever gonna leave me, and now she done left me to go die. She gone and I don't wanna stay with nobody but her."

Franky took a seat at the kitchen table, because his legs were too weak to stand on. He had dealt with so much death over the last few years, and he realized that it was one of those things he could never get used to. His heart ached for his little friend because he knew exactly how he was feeling. He was hurting as well because he really liked Mrs. Bertha. She was always so kind to him and his cousins.

"What's wrong?" Khadija asked, taking a seat beside him

at the raggedy card table that they used for their dinette set.

Franky held up a finger to her and allowed his little friend to grieve.

"If I be good, will God bring her back? I'll be good, Franky. I'll be good. I won't talk back no more. I want do nuttin' wrong. I want my grandma," Jason said, crying harder now. "Why she have to leave me? You said she was strong, Franky. You told me that she was coming home and now she gone. Tell God I'll be good."

Franky listened to his little friend and couldn't help but feel his pain. If there was a magic stick he could wave to stop the pain he was hearing over the phone, he would do it. And as much death and destruction he'd dealt with in his own short life, he didn't know what to say to Jason. He hated it when people came up to him after his mother and father died with lame lines like *Your daddy's in a better place* or *Your mother isn't suffering anymore*. Those people, although they meant well, really pissed him off. How was his father in a better place when the best place for a father to be was with his child? And how did they know if his mother had been suffering? All of these thoughts ran through his mind as he held the phone to his ear listening to how Mr. Death had broken his young friend's little heart.

"Hello?" a female's voice said into Franky's ear.

"Yes," he answered.

"Who is this?"

"This is Franky. I live across the street from Jason."

"Oh, I see," she said calmly. "Well, Jason is upset right now, so I think he needs to get some rest."

"I understand," Franky said. "Tell him I've been there, and he can call me anytime he likes."

"I don't think he'll be doing that. Have a good day," she said, and the phone went dead.

Franky pulled the phone away from his ear and looked at. "What was that all about?" he said, hanging up.

He told Khadija the details of his conversation with Jason, and she held her hand to her heart. "Aww, no," she said. "That's the little boy you're always telling me about?"

"Yeah," Franky said. "But then this lady got on the phone and basically told me he had to go and wouldn't be calling me anymore."

"I wouldn't take that too personal. Maybe she's grieving in her own little way. Some people lash out while others withdraw, and then you have some who stay in denial for-ever. Like me. I still don't believe my grandmother is dead. I just can't bring myself to believe that."

"Yeah," Franky said. "Whatever gets you through your day."

"It's kind of hard to study after hearing that," Khadija said.

"Yeah," he said. "But I need to get off on the right track, so I gotta stay focused."

There was a knock on the door, and Franky jumped up to answer it.

"Is Rico here?" asked a weird-looking girl whom Franky had never seen before.

"Who's asking?" Franky said, always on guard.

"I'm just a friend of his from Nawlins," the girl said in a low and thick Louisiana drawl. She had platinum hair that shot straight up in spikes, silver contact lenses—or maybe those were her real eyes—and African tribal scars on both cheeks. Two earrings dangled from her nostrils and at least twenty more from each earlobe. She wore a tight-fitting shirt that showed off her ample breasts and wore even tighter jeans. If she didn't look so crazy, she would be sexy. But the weirdest thing of all was the fact that she was wearing a trench coat, in the humid and hot Georgia summer.

"He's here sometimes but rarely," Franky said. "What's your name?"

"You just tell him his call got true, respect," the girl said. "I'll leave a number for him?"

"Sure," Franky said.

"Gone get something to write wit, boi? The name is Donita."

"I'll remember it."

The girl frowned but spit out the numbers and walked away. Franky walked back over to the table and wrote it down exactly like she said.

"The next time I'll suggest we study at the library," he said. "It's a million and one distractions around here."

"Who was that?" Khadija asked.

"I don't know, but she came for my cousin Rico, and he's always into something out in left field. But I think he can do better than that . . . or maybe he can't."

Khadija hunched her shoulders and smiled. "So can I but I'm here."

"No, you can't," he said. "You'd be lonely without me."

"I'm just kidding with ya, shawty," Khadija said. "I like being with you."

"I like being with you, too. I was surprised you said you would come over."

"Why?"

"I don't know. I mean, you've known me for only about a week now, and you're all up in my crib."

"I trust you, and plus I know that you can throw them thangs," she said, holding up her fist simulating a boxer's stance.

"I don't like fighting. I've had only two fights—well, if you don't count the times my cousins beat me up. That's in my whole life. My dad put me in boxing when I was young, so I still remember a few things, but I really could do without it. Fighting is for those without brains."

"I hear ya, shawty," she said. "Did you talk to Coach English today?"

"Yeah," he said. "I have him for PE. He told me I can come out for the team, but I need to get a physical first. So I gotta find somebody to take me and get one."

"I can ask my dad to take you," she said. "He wants to meet you anyway."

"That would be cool. I appreciate that."

"No problem, man."

"Finally," Franky said, throwing his hands up in celebration. "I'm a man not a shawty."

"Boy, stop," she said.

Rico burst through the front door with a mean mug on his face. He paused when he saw Khadija sitting at the table "How ya doing, lil lady?" he said with no smile.

"I'm fine," she said. "And you?"

Rico nodded.

"Khadija, this is my cousin Rico," Franky said.

"Nice to meet you, Rico," she said.

"Same here. I heard a lot about you," he said before turning to Franky. He used his index finger to call him over. "Can I talk to you for a second?"

Franky stood and walked over to Rico. They went out onto the front porch for some privacy.

"Some chick named Donita came by here looking for you."

"I don't know no Donita," Rico said. "What she look like?"

"She looked crazy. Spiked hair, scars on her face. Then she had on a coat," he said. "Hot as it is out here. She had on a full-length coat."

"And she asked for me?" he asked.

"Yeah," Franky said. "She looked scary."

Rico searched his brain, then all of a sudden he seemed to know who this crazy woman was.

"She left a number for you," Franky said. "It's in the kitchen. She said to tell you your call got through. Whatever that means."

"Okay," Rico said, nodding his head. "Cool. I'll get with her in a minute. Gotta get this money right first."

"Who is she?"

"Don't worry about it," he said, then turned away from Franky and stared across the street. He shook his head and seemed to be overwhelmed with emotion. Franky walked over and put his hand on his shoulder. "You a'ight, cuz?" he asked.

"Nah, I'm not good right now, whoadie. I'm not doing good at all. As a matter of fact, I think I'm about to lose my mind."

"What's up?" Franky asked, genuinely concerned about his cousin.

"You know Mrs. Bertha from across the street passed on," Rico said, wiping away tears.

Franky had never seen his cousin cry. Not even when his dad died and they placed his body into the ground. Nigel was a mess at the funeral, but that was to be expected. He was always the more sensible one. Rico was as hard as steel and didn't seem to have a sensible or sensitive bone in his body. But here he was standing on the porch with a face full of tears over a woman he barely spoke to.

"I know. Jason called and told me," Franky said, still baffled by his cousin's sensitivity toward the old woman.

"You know that means?" he said, and seemed to prepare himself for the words he was about the spew.

"What?"

"Nigel's charges have been upgraded. They 'bout to charge my brother with murder."

15

Franky walked down his street with Khadija. Neither one of them said much as they made their way to the MARTA bus station, a full two blocks away from his house. Khadija reached out and grabbed his hand with hers. Franky stiffened for a second but relaxed and fell into a groove with her.

The ghetto was full of life all around them as they made their way up onto Ralph David Abernathy Boulevard. The crackheads were out trying to flag down cars in order to scrape up enough money to get their next hit. The young corner boys were out in full force, hawking their poison for profit. Shorty, the midget, was still out in front of the liquor store begging.

"Young buck," he said. "Whatchu know good? Good Lord, you got good taste, young buck. How you doing, ma'am?"

"Hi," Khadija said.

"You two fine young people wouldn't happen to have a dollar or two on ya, would you?"

Franky reached into his pants pocket and pulled out a dollar. He handed it to Shorty and walked past him

"Thank ya, young buck. You all right with me. Hey, you wanna buy a lock for a dollar? I stole it off of this fool's bike who forgot to lock it. All you gotta do is go to the locksmith and have a key made."

Khadija laughed and so did Franky.

Two girls were in the McDonald's parking lot screaming at each other at the top of their lungs, acting like they wanted to fight, but neither of them made a move toward the other. Two police officers were sitting on the hood of their cruiser in the BP parking lot. Franky couldn't help but wonder if they were the ones who arrested his cousin. He used to love the police when he lived in New Orleans, but seeing how they shot first and asked questions last when they were dealing with hood people, he didn't like them anymore.

"Do you believe in curses?" he asked as they walked past the police officers.

"I don't know," she said. "I mean, people say God curses entire generations, but they also say He's a forgiving God, so I don't know. Why do you ask?"

"Because I believe I'm cursed," he said.

"No, you're not," she said, squeezing his hand tighter. "You're just going through some tough times right now. We all go through them, Franky."

"Tough times are one thing, but what I'm dealing with is a monster. I lost my mother, and although it was hard, she was sick, so we were prepared for it. My father was killed. That hurricane murdered him. He didn't die—he was killed—and you can never be prepared for that. My daddy was my best friend, ya heard. He was my daddy, but he was my best friend. We did everything together. And after he left, I swear a piece of me left, too. I can't wait to go to sleep at night so I can dream about him. There wasn't a day that went by that I didn't hear him tell me how much he loved me. Wasn't no shame in it either."

"It shouldn't be," she said.

"I lost my daddy, my uncle, and my grandma on the same day, ya heard. That damn Katrina. Now I come here and I finally start to get some sense of normalcy again and now look. My cousin is being charged with a crime he didn't have anything to do with. And the dude who should be locked up is gone in the wind. And the bad part about it is his sorry momma gonna let my cousin sit in jail. She knows who broke into Mrs. Bertha's house."

"Y'all got a lawyer, right? I mean, we got all kinds of cameras at the school. They should be able to see that your cousin brought her up there. I've never stepped a foot in a law school, and I can figure this one out."

"Yeah, but these lawyers cost money. Money that we just don't have. I may have something coming through, but it's nothing like what that lady asking for. She wants ten thousand dollars and probably more, now that it's a superior court case," Franky said, shaking his head. "Then my cousin, Rico, wants to spend the money on some crazy witch doctor or something."

"Witch doctor?" Khadija asked.

"Yeah," Franky said, shaking his head again at the situation. "He's nuts."

"What about a public defender? I mean, even one of them should be able to handle this case."

"Nah, Nigel ain't tryna chance his life to some law school D student. And besides, don't they work for the courts? So how hard are they really gonna fight to free my cousin? Prisons are big business, and they work hard to keep folks in 'em."

Khadija nodded. They made it to the bus stop, and before they could sit down, Bubba and Nard walked up.

"What's up, my peoples?" Bubba said, slapping Franky's hand and placing a wad of money in it.

Franky smoothly cuffed the money and reached over and shook Nard's hand. He turned around so that his back was away from Khadija and slid the money into his back pocket without her seeing it.

"What's up for the weekend?" Nard said. "We tryna hit this teen club out in Tucker. Studio Seventy-two. Jermaine Dupri's spot. You down?"

"Man—" Franky started, but was interrupted by his new woman.

"Nope," Khadija said. "He's gonna be with me."

"Okay, wifey," Bubba said, jumping back. "Put your foot down early. I guess you ain't going nowhere, Franky. I guess we see who runs things in that household."

"Shut up, Khadija," Nard said, walking up on her and bumping her with his stomach. "You always tryna boss somebody around. Boss me?"

"Boy, if you don't get your lil short, fat, Buddha-looking self out of my face," she said, "I will try my best to knock the black off of you."

Nard laughed and held up his shirt for the world to see his big round belly.

"Oh my goodness," Khadija said, laughing. "That is pitiful."

"You know you love it. How you gonna call me outta my name? I thought we were cool," Nard said.

"We are cool," she said.

"Man, are you coming to the club or what?" Nard asked. "I know you ain't gonna let this lil peanut-head girl run your life, is ya?"

"Somebody needs to run you around a track about fifty-five times until you lose some weight," Khadija said. "Then they need to take you to a doctor and see if they can stretch your head off of your shoulders so you can have a neck like everybody else."

"She's killing you, dog," Bubba said.

"Ain't nobody thinking about Khadija with her mean self," Nard said.

"We're out," Bubba said.

"Go on and rub it one time for good luck before I leave," Nard said, holding up his shirt again and pointing the big and round thing at Khadija.

"That's disgusting," she said. "You shouldn't have a beer gut at fifteen, Nard."

"I'm seventeen and why not?" he asked with a straight face.

"And you're still in the ninth grade? You're supposed to be like a junior or a senior. Why do you even bother coming to school?"

"There you go," Nard said, fanning her off. "I swear y'all the perfect couple. You know your man had me sitting up in class the other day taking notes. Do you know how stupid I looked taking notes?"

Franky laughed.

"Don't you tell anybody else that," Khadija said.

"I'm out," Nard said, shaking Franky's hand and reaching out to do the same for Khadija.

She narrowed her eyes at him and left his hand hanging there.

"I hope you find some kind of niceness now that you have a lil boyfriend," Nard said.

"Come on, man," Bubba called out to Nard.

"Y'all be easy," Nard said, and shuffled his big body to catch up with his partner in crime.

"That boy is crazy," Franky said as he watched his new friends walk off.

"They're bad news, Franky," she said, staring him down. "What did he give you?"

"What do you mean?" he asked, busted.

"What did you put in your back pocket?"

Franky sighed. He didn't want to lie to her, but the truth just wasn't an option. "I had to borrow some money from him so that we can pay the rent."

"And how are you going to pay it back?" she asked, sitting down on the bench.

"Rico said he would get it back to him," he lied, taking a seat beside her.

"Okay," Khadija said. "But please stay clear of them. Bubba is cool, and I really wish he would stick with basketball, but he's a lost soul. Doesn't realize that he can make legitimate money if he just focused on the right things. He'll be in jail or dead in two years."

"Yeah. You're probably right."

"And Nard will live forever. His kind don't die—they multiply," she said, shaking her head.

Franky was ready to change the subject. "I'm happy you came by today, and I'm sorry to put all of my problems on you like that. I bet you wish you never met me, huh?"

"Nah, man," she said, smiling. "I like being with you, shawty. I'm not one of those girls who run at the first sign of trouble. You're a good dude, Franky. And all of the drama you're dealing with doesn't have anything to do with choices you made."

Franky placed a hand on her leg and turned to look into her yes. "Yeah, I know, but still . . . I'm happy we are here. I'm happy to be here. With you. Sorry we didn't get much studying done."

"You're good, shawty," she said. "It's Friday. We have all weekend long to make something happen. Do not go to that club with them or I'll have to stop talking to you. I don't do thugs. I told you that when we first met."

"I'm not in a clubbing mood," he said. "Besides, I'd much rather spend my time with you than be up in some club with all those fine girls with short shorts, cleavage, and all of that other mess."

"Get knocked out, shawty," she said with a smile.

The bus came and Franky stood. He turned around to look at Khadija, who was still seated.

"This is your bus, right?" he asked.

"Yep," she said. "But I'll catch the next one. If you don't mind."

The driver opened the door and let some people off. Four more people got on. The driver looked at them and held his hand out as if to ask them what they were going to do. When no reply came, he closed the door and pulled off.

"I don't mind at all. Nothing but drama back where I'm headed. I could stay away forever, and it would be a'ight with me," Franky said, sitting back down beside her.

"Good, because I'm not ready to leave you just yet, shawty," she said, and slid closer to him. She laid her head on his shoulder.

Franky sat back and placed his arm around her shoulder, forcing her to lie on his chest.

"It's getting dark," he said. "Won't your parents be worried about you?"

"Nah," she said. "They told me to be home by ten o'clock, and it's only nine. The bus ride is only ten or fifteen minutes from here. So I have a little more time, and I'm using it all up."

"That's cool," Franky said. "So everybody is saying we are together. I guess that's true, huh?"

"I guess so, shawty," Khadija said with a smile. "You have been checked out, and you're official."

Franky smiled and pulled her a little closer. She felt good in his arms, and he realized that this was the most peace he'd felt in three years.

16

Franky sat in the living room waiting while Rico talked on the telephone with somebody. Franky could pick up bits and pieces of their conversation, and he was grateful because Rico wasn't very forthcoming with anything. Her heard Stick's name mentioned several times, and he was happy because that meant Rico wasn't sticking to the dumb no-snitching street crap. Over the last few days, he had become obsessed with finding Stick. The bum's mother wasn't answering her door for anyone, and although there was movement in the house, Stick seemed to have up and vanished into thin air.

"What did she say?" Franky asked as soon as he heard Rico say good-bye.

"Nothing," he said. "Let's go. Have you seen where I put those car keys?"

Franky shook his head and stood up. He would prefer to catch the bus because Rico's driving was atrocious. He walked out on the front porch and waited for Rico to find the keys he seemed to lose every day. He stood there, noticing how quiet the streets were for a Saturday morning. In his old neighborhood of Jefferson Parish, Saturday mornings were filled with people out in their yards working. Cutting grass, jogging, chatting with neighbors about the trials of the previous week and just enjoying the morning sun. Suddenly, all of the differences between his past life and his present were coming to mind, and he wondered why that was.

"Let's go," Rico said as he locked the door behind him.

They walked out to the car, and Franky got into the passenger's seat.

"How much money do you have now?" Rico asked.

"I have a grand," Franky said. "But I have three hundred more coming in on Monday."

"That's good," Rico said. "Let me get it."

Franky reached into his pocket and handed Rico the money.

"I know what you doing to get this money, Franky, and I know you think I don't care, but I do and I don't like it. I'm not in a position to do too much about it right now, but once this is over, I want you to stop, ya heard?"

"I don't want any part of it, either, so that ain't no problem," Franky said, not even bothering to try covering up his new gig.

"I also know that you gave dem boys some cash to get started. Now, I'm gonna ask you one more time. How much money did you get from that so-called backyard find?"

Franky huffed. "I got six hundred dollars, and I didn't find it in the backyard. This dude was running from you and Stick, and he jumped in my window. He gave me the six hundred because I hid him from y'all. I gave Nigel half to pay the rent, and I gave the other three to them dudes at school to make this money for Nigel's lawyer. That's the truth."

"You hid him?" Rico snapped. "Let me tell you somethin', lil whoadie. We family and family don't take food outta each other's mouths. You might not like what I do, but you don't ever go against me, ya heard?"

"Man," Franky said, "that boy was scared to death. I would've wanted somebody to do that for me, so I just put myself in his shoes."

"Yeah, but it wasn't you. Like I said, don't ever go against family. And if that's the case, why did you lie?"

"Because I'm tired of being hungry all the time, and I didn't want to give you the money because you know how you get all these crazy ideas, and the next thing you know the money is gone, and we're back to eating red beans and rice every night. I'm tired of my ribs touching my back, so I kept the other money so I could eat," Franky said.

Rico looked at his cousin and for the first time in his entire life, he showed some compassion. He reached over and tapped Franky's leg. "I understand, whoadie. We've been tryna do the right thing so we can stay together, but tough times call for touch moves, ya heard. I'm sorry 'bout going off on ya. I'm a desperate man right 'bout now."

"It's cool," Franky said. He looked out the window at two pit bulls. The dogs were standing guard beside some guy's shiny car. "Who was that girl who came by the house looking for you? The weird-looking one," Franky asked.

Rico smiled. "That's my secret weapon. Made a call down to Louisiana and got me a bayou geechie girl. She's from South Carolina and Louisiana. They say she was born in Carolina, died at birth, and when they crossed over into Louisiana, which is where they were taking her to bury, she found a heartbeat. She was raised deep in the swamps. Smarter than you but never stepped foot into a school building. She gone flush Stick out of whatever hole he's hiding in. She's costing a pretty penny, too."

"How are we gonna pay a lawyer and some witch doctor?" Franky said.

"Forget them lawyers. They all in cahoots together. They stay making side deals with each other. If you got money, then you can be a'ight in the system, but if you poor like us, they 'bout to getcha. Plus, you only need a lawyer when you guilty. You need a geechie woman when you're innocent."

Franky frowned. He hated when Rico started thinking. He was about the dumbest person in America, and his wild, harebrained ideas always put Franky in a bad mood.

"So, what if she can't find him? We just lose the money and Nigel stays in jail?"

"The geechie girl gone come through. They never fail, ya heard. She gone make that fool an offer he can't refuse," Rico said, nodding. "There people in this world you don't know nuttin' 'bout, whoadie. And Geechie Girl is one of them. She will have him in her grasp in no time. Let me handle this."

Franky prayed silently that God would release Nigel and find a brain for Rico. He looked over at his cousin who was biting his bottom lip so hard Franky thought he was going to draw blood. Rico turned up the radio and listened to the new Mystikal song that they were playing in heavy rotation. As the New Orleans rapper yelled about a girl with a real big butt, Rico bobbed his head to the beat until they made it to the Atlanta City Jail.

Rico pulled into the parking lot of Free at Last Bail Bondsman and almost hit a car. Franky shook his head, thanking God for allowing them to arrive in one piece. They got out of the car and started walking toward the jail when someone yelled, "Yo."

"What's up?" Rico said, turning around.

"Y'all can't park there unless y'all using us to bail somebody out."

"We would love to bail him out, but he ain't got no bail," Rico said.

Ain't got no bail, Franky thought. *What kind of way is that to talk to businesspeople?*

"Come on in," the man said. "Let me see what I can do for ya. I got people over there who might be able to bend a few rules."

Rico turned to Franky. "You go ahead and handle the visit. I'ma see what this dude is talking about. Tell Nigel I got a call in to the bayou. That might lift his spirits."

"Since when did we get money to be paying a lawyer, a witch doctor, and a bail bondsman?" Franky said.

"Let me handle this, boy," Rico said, balling a fist and threatening to punch him.

Franky threw his hands up and ran across the street, up the steps of the Atlanta City Jail, and into the lobby. Once inside, he signed the visitors' list and waited for his name to be called.

He sat on the hard plastic chairs of the waiting room, flipping through outdated magazines and half watching the television that was mounted up in the corner of the large room. ESPN was on and they were talking about the New Orleans Saints. He missed going to the games with his dad and uncle.

"Franky Bourgeois."

He turned away from the screen when he heard his name being called over the intercom. He stood and walked back to where an old security guard was standing with a clipboard.

"You Franky?" the old man asked.

"Yes, sir," he said.

"Follow me."

Franky walked behind the slow-moving man until they came to an orange door. The old man scanned a card, and the hard steel door clicked and opened. The guard pulled and pointed inside.

"Have a seat at booth number seven," the guard said. "He will be with you in just a second."

Franky walked in and the big door closed behind him. He wasn't sure why but he was afraid. He had never been inside of a jail before. He took a seat at booth number seven and looked around. There was a really thick glass that someone had tried to carve their initials on. Gang signs and other forms of graffiti were all over the walls of the booth. Franky sat fidgeting with the phone on the wall while he waited for his cousin to come out.

Nigel walked in and smiled. He sat down across from Franky and lifted the receiver. He had on an oversized navy blue jumpsuit, and his hair was growing wildly. His face was covered with a beard.

"What's up, whoadie?" he said with a huge smile on his face. "How you doing?"

"I'm all right," Franky said. "What a difference a couple of weeks can make. Look at you."

"Yeah," Nigel said, rubbing his head. "I need a shave and a haircut bad. Where is Rico?"

"He went to talk to some bail bondsman across the street. Man, that dude is crazy. He wants to spend our money on some witch doctor from New Orleans. Geechie something."

Nigel frowned but didn't say anything. He just hunched his shoulders as if Rico's way was a viable option.

Franky was amazed at how good of spirits he seemed to be in. He couldn't help but think of how depressing it had to be to sit in jail for a crime you didn't commit.

"That boy," Nigel said. "He thinks he can make up his own rules. I've been thinking real hard 'bout Mrs. Bertha and lil Jason. Have you spoken with him?"

"Yeah, he called, but his auntie or somebody hung up on me."

"They probably think I had something to do with Mrs. Bertha's death. You can't blame them too much. Especially if they listening to these lying police, ya heard."

"Yeah," Franky said. "I guess you're right."

"I keep thinking that maybe I shouldn't have said anything about Stick being in her house. I should've just went after him myself and had lil Jason put the stuff back. Maybe she would still be with us, ya know," Nigel said. "She was a sweet lady."

"Did you tell the lawyer that it was Stick? I mean, forget that no-snitching bullcrap. This isn't a petty theft. This is real."

"Yeah, I told her, but she wants a lot of money. I mean a lot. This is a murder case now."

"So whatchu gonna do?" Franky asked.

"I think I'll be okay," Nigel said with a smile.

"Why you smiling?" Franky asked as if his cousin had finally snapped and lost his mind.

"I just found out where Stick is," he said.

"Where is he?"

"Right in here," he said, nodding. "Came in early this morning they say. Ain't been able to touch him yet, but I got the goons on it. Cuz, they got so many cats up in here from Nawlins. It's like a lil homecoming up in here. But I ain't tryna get too comfortable, ya heard."

Franky couldn't help but smile. This was great news. He didn't care how they got Stick to confess as long as his cousin wasn't facing a murder charge.

"What's up with this young lady who has your nose all open?" Nigel asked.

"Yeah." Franky smiled. "She's cool."

"She's cool," Nigel said sarcastically. "Yeah, right. She's more than cool. Got my lil cuz cheesing from ear to ear. Look at you. It's all good, whoadie. I like love."

"I got my classes changed, too. I'm out of the dumb group. And my new classes are a whole lot more like real school."

"What were the other ones like?"

"A zoo. They had had so many clowns in there that the teacher couldn't teach. All she did was fuss at fools all day. I'm still tryna figure out why getting a laugh is so important to them."

"That's just how it is, whoadie," Nigel said. "Ya see, Uncle Frank always stressed education to you, so you look at it differently than these kids. Most of these ghetto kids wasn't raised like that. They go to school just to get out of da house. And you gotta understand that life is hard in the ghetto, so when they get a chance to have some fun, they do it. If you ain't never had nobody tell you how to be a student, you won't know how. And by the time they get to high school, it's a wrap. Too late."

"Yeah, well, thank God for my mom and dad," Franky said.

"Yeah," Nigel said. "The good Lord looked out for you. I'm proud of you, whoadie. We should've got you back in school a long time ago."

"Yeah, but it's cool. I'm gonna be playing football, too," Franky said.

"What position they gonna put you at?"

"I don't know," Franky said. "Been so long since I played I might be the water boy."

"Nah. Our family is full of athletes. My daddy played, yo daddy played, I even heard our granddaddy played baseball, and all of us played. So you'll be fine, whoadie."

Nigel's name was called, and he shot his head around and looked at the huge guard whose shirt was far too tight.

"What's up?" Nigel said with a frown.

"Visit is over," the guard said with a smirk on his face. "Time's up."

"Are you serious? My people just got here," Nigel protested. "I'm talking not even five minutes."

"Time's up," the guard barked as his smile was replaced by a menacing scowl. "You can get up or I can come help you up."

"I think I'ma need a lil help," Nigel snapped, finally showing the signs of a man stressed out from being wrongly incarcerated.

"Are you sure that's what you want?" the guard said, walking toward Nigel. "That can be painful."

"Painful for you, potna," Nigel said. "I'm begging you to put your hands on me."

"Nigel," Franky called out. "Just go, man. It's okay. We'll be back up here to see you tomorrow."

The guard walked over and stood behind Nigel. He cracked his knuckles. "Get up, punk," the guard said.

Franky's heart skipped a beat. He knew his cousin wasn't the type of guy to let this kind of disrespect slide. He also knew he wasn't going to just sit there and get beat up. This was going to be a fight—a very brutal fight—because although Nigel was easygoing, he was hell on wheels once his temper got the best of him. And all that meant was there would be more charges added onto the bogus ones he already had.

Nigel stood and faced the guard. Both men's eyes blazed and they sized each other up.

The guard held out both of his hands as if to ask Nigel what he was going to do.

Nigel didn't say anything, nor did he move one step back. His chest was rising and falling at a rapid pace.

"Get your butt outta here and go pack your things," the guard said. "You outta here."

"What?" Nigel asked, still on edge. "What did you just say?"

"Don't ask questions, Bourgeois," the guard said with a smile. "Just get your tail up outta here before I tell them to lose your paperwork. You know it'll take another two or three days before we get around to finding it. Then you'll be stuck in here with me."

"Don't want that," Nigel said.

"Wait a minute," the guard said. "How you gonna try to fight me? I thought we were cool?"

"We're cool, man," Nigel said, smiling and shaking the guard's hand. "We're cooler than a fan."

"I guess the clown who did that crime they had you in here for decided to find Jesus. He singing like a bird, but on himself. In all my years of being a CO, I never seen anything like it. The boy is shook. Something got him scared out of his mind," the guard said.

Nigel smiled, turned to Franky, and said, "Geechie girl got him."

Franky sat there with his mouth open. He was stunned as he watched his cousin slap the guard on the back and walk out of the side door.

Franky pulled himself together and stood. He walked over to the big orange door that he had just entered and pressed the little silver button. The door clicked open, and he walked out. He was happy to be leaving this place but even happier that his cousin Nigel would be going with him.

17

Franky was sitting at the desk in Khadija's mother's office, which was really a converted bedroom, playing a game on his cell phone. Now that he had become business partners with Bubba and Nard, he had a few extra dollars to join the cellular crowd. They had just finished studying for their Spanish test and were trying to think of something else to do.

"I have an idea," Khadija said, standing up from her position on the sofa by the window.

"What?"

"Let's go out to Stone Mountain Park," she suggested.

"What? Why?"

"Because you need to get in shape, dude. Coach English is no joke. And unless you want to be sitting on the bench the whole season, you need to get your butt in shape. You're already behind the power curve, shawty."

"Why can't we just go over to the school and use the track?" Franky asked.

"Because we're always at school, and I need a new scene. Have you ever been to Stone Mountain Park?"

"Nope," he said.

"Then that's a good enough reason. It's five miles around the mountain, and it's really pretty out there, lots of colorful flowers and everything," she said.

Whenever Khadija said things like that, it always took him by surprise since his initial impression of her was that of a hard girl.

"Isn't Stone Mountain supposed to be where those Ku Klux Klan fools live?"

"Man," Khadija said, fanning him off. "That was back in the sixties. Like when my momma and daddy were two years old. You'd be hard pressed to find a white person out there now, let alone a Ku Klux Klan member. Stone Mountain has been blacked out."

"Oh, okay. Well, I'm down like four flats," Franky said. "I need to go home and change into some workout clothes."

"Duh," Khadija said, rolling her eyes. "I didn't expect you to go running in those shell toes and skinny jeans. You would look like a complete fool."

"You're always getting smart with somebody," he said, balling up a piece of paper and throwing it at her. He missed.

"I hope you're not trying to play quarterback, throwing like that."

Franky walked over and picked up the paper. He faked left, then right, and shot the paper in the wastebasket by the desk. "Five, four, three, two, one . . . swish," he said with his hand up in the air with a follow-through as the wad of paper hit the bottom of the can. "Game. I need to play basketball. The game is sick."

"Ahh," Khadija said. "I've seen you play basketball, so . . . no, you don't."

Franky laughed. "Hater. I'm a little rusty but give me a lil bit of time, whoadie. I'll be like Chris Paul up in there."

Khadija looked at one of her many colorful G-Shock watches. "It's almost one o'clock now," she said. "I'll meet you in front of the school in an hour. Then we can catch the train out to Stone Mountain. Is that cool?"

"Why can't I just wait for you and we go together?" he said. "It's not gonna take me that long to get dressed."

"That's fine. I'll go get changed."

"Five miles, Khadija? I need to ease into getting in shape. You're tryna kill me."

"No, I'm not," she said. "Let me go get into my workout gear. I need to be back here by seven to eat."

Franky walked over to his girlfriend, reached out, and gave her a hug. He liked touching her; he liked being in her presence. To put it plainly, he liked everything about her. As he held her in his arms, he looked down into her eyes. She stared back up at him and smiled.

"I have something to tell you," he said with a serious expression on his face.

"What?" she asked with a worried one on hers.

"Your breath is kicking it," he said, fanning his nose.

Khadija pulled away and punched him in the arm.

Franky rubbed his arm, getting the sting out. He looked at her and couldn't stop smiling.

"Whatchu smiling about?" Khadija asked.

"You," he said.

"Okay. Let me go get dressed, shawty."

Finally. He was happy.

He was back in school, his cousin was home from jail,

and he had the most popular female freshman at M&M High School as his girlfriend.

"What are you two lovely people doing in here?" Mrs. Davis, Khadija's mom, said as she hurried into the office and searched her filing cabinet for something.

"We were studying, but now that we're done, Mrs. Track Star over there wants to go running around Stone Mountain. And she said it's five miles."

"Yeah, but it's a pretty five miles," Mrs. Davis said. "Your dad is cooking out tonight, so make sure you're back by six or seven," she said to Khadija.

"I know," she said.

"Well, make sure you're not late since you know."

"Franky, you are more than welcome to come back and have dinner with us."

Mrs. Davis looked like an older version of her daughter. The only exception was she was lighter in complexion and a little heavier in the hips. She was cordial to Franky and seemed to be feeling him out.

"That sounds like music to my ears," he said. "I doubt you'll ever hear me turn down a home-cooked meal."

"Good," she said, and retrieved the paperwork she was trying to find, smiled at him and Khadija, then walked out.

Franky wished his parents could've met Khadija's family. He could see all of them sitting on the deck of their huge house in New Orleans overlooking the water while his dad and Mr. Davis talked shop over a smoking grill. Khadija was exactly the kind of girl his dad talked about.

I like people who are from the hood but who never let the hood define them, he would often say.

Khadija fit that bill. She was serious about her schoolwork and her future. She was truly her own woman, and her parents gave her lots of freedom because she had proved time and time again that she could handle it. Both of her parents were cool, but Mr. Davis treated Franky like he was a member of the family. Franky often felt like he was talking to his own dad when they sat around and had their chats. Mrs. Davis was a workaholic and had a mean streak in her, but there was no doubt how much she loved her children. She was an elementary school teacher but moonlighted as an income tax preparer. Mr. Davis was a military man and was often out of the country doing his soldier thing. They both had a love for football, and when Mr. Davis picked him up and took him to get his football physical, they were connected from that point on. Mr. Davis was a diehard University of Georgia fan and even named their family dog UGA.

Franky walked around the converted office and looked at the family pictures that lined the bookshelves. There were all kinds of pictures of Khadija in all phases of her life. He picked up a picture of Khadija taken when she was around four or five years old. Both of her front teeth were missing, yet she was smiling for the world to see. He smiled when he looked at her. She had a million and one different color beads in her hair. Times change but some things stay the same.

18

Franky and Khadija sat beside each other on the MARTA bus, laughing to themselves at the passengers. Khadija pointed out a man who was sitting across from them wearing a tight-fitting one-piece jumpsuit and some platform shoes that were straight out of the seventies. He was skinny and had on a large set of headphones that had probably been popular in the seventies as well.

"He has to be going to a party," Khadija said. "Please tell me he's going to a party and this is not his everyday attire."

"I think the brother looks fly. Super Fly. I'ma get me one of those outfits for our prom."

"Who you going with?"

"You," Franky said.

Super Fly wasn't paying them any attention. He was bobbing his head to the beat of whatever he was listening to. Then out of the blue, he yelled out the James Brown tune he was listening to, then started fanning himself.

"That's right," Khadija said, laughing. "Cool yoself down."

"Go over there and wake up your auntie," Franky said, nodding toward a woman who was asleep. Her large wig was tilted to the side, and she was nodding back and forth. Her mouth was open, and when her head tilted back too far, she would open her eyes, close her mouth, and look around to see who was watching.

They couldn't control their laughter when she turned her attention to them. The old woman twisted up her lip and turned her body away from them in her seat.

The skinny singer's song must've gotten good to him, and he yelled out another verse.

"He is killing that banana-yellow one-piece suit," she said.

"Maybe he has a show. I don't know—that's your family," Franky joked.

"He looks just like you," Khadija said. "Look at his lips. Y'all gotta be related."

"Then his Jheri curl juice is dripping on the seats," Franky said. "He's gonna mess around and make somebody slip and fall."

They were enjoying themselves way too much and had just found another target to laugh at when the driver stopped, and it was time for them to get off. Franky gave the skinny singer a thumbs-up before exiting the bus.

"I'm glad you said good-bye to your people," Khadija said. "You're so polite, Franky."

"Yeah," Franky said. "My future uncle-in-law."

They were laughing as if they didn't have a care in the world when all of a sudden, Franky heard footsteps coming up behind them. Something told him to turn around, and just as he twisted his head to the left, a fist came flying at his face. The blow landed flush between his eyes, knocking him off balance. He hit the ground, and his head slammed into the pavement. The pain was instant and caused him to temporarily black out. He heard Khadija yell and looked up to see her throwing wild punches and screaming profanities at her assailant. Then he didn't hear her anymore and saw her fall backward. He tried to get up to help her, but his attackers were on him in no time. They were like a pack of hungry hyenas as they pummeled him from all angles. Fists with rings on them found his head, face, and chest. Steel-toed Timberland boots rained down on his back, legs, and buttocks. Franky was getting hit and kicked in every place imaginable, yet he kept his hands over his head. He counted three different people while covering himself. But as he was being pummeled by this pack of maniacs, his only concern was for Khadija. Where was she? He couldn't see her anymore, and that caused him to panic, but every time he tried to get up, he was kicked and more punches battered his body. He tried to make out what the boys were saying while they attacked him, but nothing registered. He stayed covered up in the fetal position on the sidewalk and tried to wait out the assault. He saw his own blood on the pavement, but he couldn't do anything but try to protect his head. He felt someone tugging at his pants pockets, and he was thankful that he had only ten dollars on him. He felt his cell phone leave his possession. There was a loud boom, and just as sudden as the assault started, it was over.

He heard a familiar voice yell at the boys as they laughed and ran off. Franky slowly removed his hands from his head and tried to get his mind right. He slowly pulled himself to an upright position. He was dizzy and had trouble

balancing himself even while sitting down. He looked to
his left, then his right, searching for Khadija, but instead of
seeing his girlfriend, he stared straight into the eyes of the
midget, Shorty.

"Good Lord, young blood," Shorty said, holding a gun
that was almost as big as he was. "Somebody's mighty mad
at you."

Franky grimaced in pain. His head was throbbing, and
he instinctively reached up to massage his temples. His lip
was leaking blood like a faucet, and his mind went back to
when someone's boot connected with his mouth. He
could feel his right eye closing and swelling. He rolled
over onto his knees and tried to get to his feet. He had to
find Khadija. Where was she? He adjusted his head so that
he could see better, because the vision in his right eye was
already gone due to the swelling. While he was down on
his hands and knees, he looked up and saw some boys
running away. He zeroed in on their backs, trying desper-
ately to make out something about them that he could use
later to identify them and settle the score. All he could see
were their backs, but then one of them stopped and
turned around. He stared at Franky, threw his fingers up
in the peace sign, then turned his hand upside down, the
symbol kids used to represent the *A* for "Atlanta." The boy,
whom Franky had never seen before, smiled, then turned
his hand upright and gave Franky the finger. Franky's
anger got the best of him, and he tried to stand but his
body wasn't ready for that. He slumped back down on the
ground and took a few deep breaths to stabilize himself.
Once he could halfway think straight, he looked around
for Khadija. The insides of his Levi's pockets were inside
out, and his shell-toe Adidas were gone.

Franky found himself sitting on the sidewalk in a woozy haze. He was robbed, beaten, shoeless, and unable to locate his girlfriend. For the first time in his life, he knew what it felt like to want to kill another human being.

"I sure hate to let this thing off unless I really need to, but I'm too old to be fighting with them young boys," Shorty said. "You need me to help you up, young blood?"

How are you gonna help me up, Shorty? I'm sitting down, and I'm still taller than you, Franky thought.

"Where's Khadija?" Franky said, rolling onto his knees again as blood squirted from his nose and mouth.

"Oh, Lord," Shorty said, running away from Franky and over to a lone figure lying on the ground by a trash can.

Franky saw her. He found the strength to get up, and he staggered over to her. He looked down, and his rage, which was already at an extremely unhealthy level, went off the charts.

"No," he said, looking down at his girl, who was lying facedown on the pavement in her own blood. She wasn't moving, and that sent him into major panic mode.

"Khadija," he said as he dropped down on his knees beside her. He started shaking her while calling her name.

"Don't move her," Shorty said, as if he had some medical training. "Gimme that cell phone."

Franky reached over and slid the iPhone from Khadija's workout armband. He handed it to Shorty.

"What the . . . ," Shorty said. "Where the numbers at?"

Franky took the phone from him and promptly dialed 911.

"That's a crying shame," Shorty said, shaking his huge head. "These young boys done lost whatever minds they had. I couldn't understand them whipping up on you—

you a man. But this a lady. In my day, a man didn't put his hands on a lady."

Franky gave the 911 operator the information about the assault and the location. All the while, Khadija still hadn't moved. Her eyes were closed and she was breathing, but that was all.

"Doggone cowards," Shorty said, frowning up. "I shoulda shot 'em all. In my day, a man fought another man straight up. If you lost, you just lost. So what. You kept it moving, but not now. Nowadays you got cowards who are too scared to take a whipping. They run and get a gun or come in packs. Three fools on one man and then they had the nerve to hit a girl. I don't know what this world is coming to."

Franky wasn't listening to Shorty's rant. He was holding on to his girlfriend's hand and praying that she would be okay. With his free hand, he scrolled through Khadija's phone until he came to MOM. He pressed the CALL button, and Mrs. Davis answered.

"Mrs. Davis," he said through his tears. "This is Franky. Khadija's hurt. Somebody jumped us when we got off the bus."

"Hurt," Mrs. Davis said. "Where is she? What kind of hurt? What do you mean she's hurt? Put her on the phone."

"She's not moving," Franky said, and the mere fact that he said that sent a shock through his entire body. "She's just lying here."

"Noooooooooo!" Mrs. Davis screamed.

"We called the ambulance already. They are on their way."

"Where are you?"

Franky told the distraught woman their location.

"I'm on my way," she said, and hung up.

Franky rubbed his girl's hand to comfort her while they waited for the paramedics to arrive. His mind was calming down and his pain no longer mattered. The only thing that was on his mind was finding out who was responsible for this and making them pay.

19

Franky sat alone staring at the ambulance as the big square truck drove his girl and her mother away. He had refused any medical attention for fear that Children's Services would come in and start asking questions. He felt like he would be okay anyway. His wounds were all on the surface, and he didn't think he had any broken bones that would require a doctor's attention.

After the taillights of the ambulance disappeared out of his view, he walked home.

"Where ya been, whoadie?" Nigel asked while lying on the sofa reading a magazine. "Hanging out with that gurl, huh? Yeah, she got ya nose open."

Franky didn't respond. Anger had a death grip on him and wouldn't let go. He was so concerned with Khadija that his heart was pounding a million beats per second. She regained consciousness after the paramedics showed up but had complained of a severe headache. There was a large knot on her forehead and a scuff mark on her cheek.

She kept calling his name, but Mrs. Davis made her be quiet.

Nigel lowered the magazine when he didn't get a response. He stared at his cousin and almost leaped from the sofa.

"What the . . . ," he said, tossing the magazine aside. "What happened to you?"

Franky looked at his cousin and his only response was a blank stare. He had never felt this way—violated, used, and mistreated. As he stared at Nigel, he thought about how people treated him. They showed him respect because he showed them kindness that was backed by the threat of violence. People were flat out afraid of Rico simply because of the level of violence that he was willing to bring their way. But what about him? Why was he feeling the disrespect of his peers? Why did he have to act like an uncivilized beast just to have some peace? He never did anything to anyone. As a matter of fact, the only thing he ever tried to do was help people; yet here he stood beaten like a runaway slave. But even worse than that was the disrespect they showed him by attacking his girlfriend. Things had to change, and he knew exactly how he was going to change them. On his walk home, he had plenty of time to think about his revenge, and he planned on serving it hotter than a New Orleans summer.

"I'm talking to you, whoadie," Nigel said, walking closer to his cousin. "What happened?"

"It's nothing," Franky said, and walked to his bedroom.

"Where ya shoes at, man?" Nigel asked with a pained expression on his face as if he could feel Franky's wounds.

Franky didn't respond. He walked into his room and sat on the side of the bed. He wanted to cry, but what good would that do? Would crying make Khadija okay? Would it heal his scars? Would it take that disdainful look off of Mrs. Davis's face when she stood on the back of the ambulance and barked, "I think it's time that you kept your distance from my daughter."

"Franky," Nigel said from the doorway. "I need to know what happened to you, man. Were you jumped, robbed? Come on, whoadie. Talk to me."

"I'm a'ight," Franky said as he lay down on his bed. "I just fell."

"Fell down and lost your shoes, too?" Nigel said. "Come on, whoadie. I was born at night but not last night. Tell me what happened. You know I'ma find out anyway."

"I'm okay," Franky said, refusing to give up any information. He was tired of his cousins handling things for him while he played the good suburban kid. The days in Jefferson Parish were gone. He didn't have a country club membership, or a pool out back. He was no longer that person. He was in the hood where only the strong survived. He had held on to the person he once was for as long as he could, but times had changed and it was about time that he changed with them.

Nigel stood there staring at his cousin. He must've read Franky's mind, because all he did was nod and step away from the bedroom door.

"I'll get you some ice for that eye," Nigel said from the hallway.

Franky felt something in his back pocket. He reached back and felt Khadija's cell phone.

"Dag it," he snapped at himself. "Now how am I gonna call her?"

He sat up and pressed a button, and the device came to

life. A picture of the two of them flashed on the screen. He flipped his fingers around the touch screen, and different pictures popped up. She had lots of photos of him that he never even knew she had. She had taken all kinds of random shots. There were pictures of him studying, walking down the hallway, and talking to his teachers. She even had one of him sleeping with his mouth open.

Franky flipped over to her text messages. He didn't want to be nosy or untrusting because that wasn't the case. He just wanted to feel connected to her. There were a bunch of text messages between the two of them, and since he already knew what they said, he skipped around until he found one from her best friend, D'Asia. Franky hadn't met Khadija's BFF yet because she attended another school, but he had talked to her on the phone a few times and they were cool.

D'Asia: Let me guess, you're with Franky.
Khadija: How did you know? LOL
D'Asia: Don't tell me my girl is in love.
Khadija: Okay. I won't say nuttin' then.
D'Asia: LOL. I can't wait to meet him.
Khadija: I can't get enuf of that N.O. slang.
D'Asia: You sprung. Can't believe u wit a M&M dude.
Khadija: He's not an M&M dude. He's different. No thug but I feel safe with him.

Franky clicked the screen off. She wasn't safe with him. He had failed to protect her, and that made him feel like a punk. He closed his eyes and tried to calm himself down.

"Hi, son."

Franky jerked his head toward the door. He jumped up

but couldn't move. Just as clear as Nigel had been stand-ing in the doorway a few minutes ago, his father stood there now.

Franklin Bourgeois Sr. smiled at his son. *"How are you doing?"*

Franky couldn't take his eyes off his dad, yet he couldn't move toward him. He tried to lift his arms, but he couldn't do that either.

His dad looked exactly as he had three years ago. He wore a baby-blue dress shirt without the tie, shiny silver cuff links, a pair of nicely creased dress slacks, and some of the shiniest shoes in the world. They were glowing.

"My, you have grown so much. I've been watching you, but I wasn't expecting this. I know life has been very dif-ferent for you, but I prepared you for this. You can handle this. This life you're living is only temporary. Life down here is about choices, and I want you to know that your mother and I weren't too happy about your choice not to go to school all that time. But we are both happy that you are back and seem to have not missed a beat. I'm over it. I can't tell you how much I miss being around you, buddy. But we'll be together again. Your mother is great, and we still have the best time together. There are lots of our family members around. Your grandmother, Rosa, is still fussing and cooking for everyone that she sees. Why are you looking at me like that?"

"Dad, can you hear me?" Franky said.

"Of course I can hear you. I can see you, too."

"Why can't I move?"

Franky Sr. smiled but didn't answer his son. Instead he continued talking. *"Life is hard down here and even harder for a teen. I can't tell you how proud I am of Nigel for taking care of you. Nigel has been a grown man about this whole ordeal."*

"Believe it or not, Rico has helped a lot, too."

"I'm not familiar with that name. Who is Rico?"

"My cousin, your nephew," Franky said. "Rico."

"Not sure who you're talking about, but listen. I don't have much time."

"Why haven't you come to see me before?"

"Well, it's complicated. You have no idea what I had to go through to get here now, but that's too long of a story. You need to hear from me. Now is a very critical time in your life, son. Choices, choices, choices. You have to make good ones, because bad ones will forever alter your life. You cannot respond to the boys who jumped you. Move on. Leave it alone. Now, I understand where you live and the rules that you live by, but you have to think. You've plotted to do some things that will get you sent to prison, Franky. And why? Because you're upset and hurt. The guys who did this are lost little boys who are projecting their hurt onto others."

"So what should I do?"

"You have to make that decision on your own. But don't go with your first choice. If you do, I won't ever be able to see you again, and all of my thoughts and memories of you will go away. You will cross over. So you are at the crossroads."

"What is that?"

Franky heard the front door open, and he turned his head for a second. When he turned back, his father had disappeared. He sat up on the side of the bed and stomped his foot in anger. His heart was racing, and he replayed the conversation he had just had. He couldn't stop looking around for his father, but he was nowhere to be found.

"Here," Nigel said, handing Franky a ziplock bag filled with ice. "Put that over ya eye, whoadie. Now, I'ma give you some time to yoself, but we gonna talk about this, ya heard?"

Franky was still stunned from seeing his father. That hadn't been a hallucination; his dad had really been there.

"You hear me?" Nigel asked.

"Okay," Franky said. He kicked his legs up on the bed and got horizontal, but rest wouldn't be coming.

"Who the hell is Tyrone?" Rico said as he burst through the door with murder in his eyes.

"Dude I got in a fight with at school," Franky said. His head couldn't take the noise of Rico's ranting and raving, so he just answered his questions.

"So he gonna get some fools and jump you? Then they beat up ya lady," Rico said with his chest rising and falling in anger. "Shorty just told me what happened."

Franky nodded and looked away. He was ashamed even though he knew this could've happened to anyone.

"We gonna handle this," Rico said with a rage Franky had never seen before. "I'm 'bout sick and tired of these Atlanta boys acting like we weak."

"We gone handle it," Nigel said calmly.

"Nah," Rico screamed at his brother. "Not yo way. My way! It's time I show 'em how we do in the Calliope. Third Ward, ya heard me."

And with that Rico left the house. There would be no calming him down. He was in gladiator mode, and once he was there, he wasn't stopping until he was completely satisfied.

20

Franky sat on the steps of his house staring up at the moon. He had been trying to clear his mind of all the chaos that had taken up permanent residence there, and sitting outside on a warm night in Georgia usually did the trick. But that wouldn't be the case tonight. His thoughts were constantly on Khadija. He had called her house so many times that her parents changed their number. After that, he decided to go by there only to have the door slammed in his face. Then to add insult to injury, Mrs. Davis opened the door before he could get off the porch and told him in a very calm and cool tone, "If you ever come back over here again, I will have you arrested for trespassing and harassment."

Franky stood there on the verge of tears and listened as the lady dressed him down with her words. Once she had slammed the door, he walked away. He took one last look up at Khadija's room on the second floor and was so happy when he saw her sitting on the windowsill looking down at him. He wasn't sure how she felt about him, since he hadn't heard from her, but she waved and then got up and walked away.

His heart ached to touch her, to be around her, to hear her voice as he stood there staring at her. It had been five whole days since the attack, and each day without speaking to her was ten times more agonizing than any Timberland boot to the face.

Franky kept looking up into the sky hoping it would rain. He was depressed, and he wanted it to rain. The rain took his family away, and he was hoping they would come and take him to join them.

He picked up Khadija's cell phone and called her friend D'Asia.

"D'Asia," he said. "This is Franky. Sorry to call you so late."

"It's okay," she said. "What's up? And when are you going to give Khadija her phone back?"

"I went to take it to her, but I got cussed out."

"Yeah," she said, "your name is mud in that house, dude."

"Khadija doesn't like me anymore, does she?"

"I don't know. She's just confused. I think she still likes you, but her mom is outraged. And Khadija will never go against her wishes."

"But why are they so mad at me? I was jumped, too," Franky pleaded.

"Yeah, but they heard something about you, Franky. And Mrs. Davis is sharp. She must believe what she heard."

"What did she hear?"

"Somebody told her that you sold drugs. Khadija said she was suspicious of the money you had, and you know

how she feels about thugs. She's heartbroken, Franky. I
don't think she really believes that you would sell drugs,
but she's not sure. But Mrs. Davis said she's one hundred
percent sure."

Franky was stunned and wondered who could've told
her something like that.

"She won't take my calls. She knows I have her phone,
and she won't even call it."

"Franky," D'Asia said. "How have you been doing? I
heard you got beat up pretty bad."

"I'm a'ight. It was nothing but a few bruises."

"Have you been to school?"

"No, I haven't, but I heard that Khadija doesn't go there
anymore."

"Why haven't you been going to school, Franky?"

"I just needed some time to think—that's all. And being
that Khadija is not there, I just wasn't in the mood. Why
did her parents pull her out of M and M?"

"I don't know, but she's at some other school in another county. I can't tell you which one, because they asked
me not to."

"I understand," Franky said.

"Mr. Davis got the video from outside of the store
where y'all got jumped, and they got the boys. They're all
locked up."

"Oh, yeah?"

"Yeah. The one named Tyrone is the only juvenile, but
he has some adult charges because he had a roll of quarters in his hand when he hit Khadija."

So it was Tyrone who hit Khadija, he thought. His
anger caused him to shake.

"The other boys are in the real jail because they are older."

"That's good. That's where they belong," Franky said calmly.

"I agree."

"Hey, listen," Franky said. "Do you mind if I call you every now and then to check up on Khadija?"

"Yeah, that's fine," D'Asia said. "Khadija is my best friend, and she doesn't like too many people. When I tell you that girl is mean, I'm not lying. But she loved you."

"And I loved her," Franky said. "I still do. Will you tell her that?"

"Of course, shawty," D'Asia said, forcing Franky to smile and wish that it was his girl calling him that.

"Okay, D'Asia," Franky said. "I appreciate you. Tell Khadija I'm thinking about her all the time."

"She knows. Trust me, she knows. I'll talk to you later, Franky. Get some rest."

"I will. Bye."

Franky hung up the phone, and all of his rage was aimed at Tyrone. He blamed him for all of this foolishness. His life was finally getting on the right track, and this fool decided he wanted to play "my city against your city" and ruin everything. Now he was about to pay. The one person he found some joy with no longer wanted anything to do with him, and he blamed Tyrone. It was time he paid the piper.

Franky took a deep breath and stood. He stretched his long body and started walking down the street. It was twelve o'clock in the morning, and there was a full moon out. He looked up into the heavens so that if his dad was looking down at him, he could see directly into his eyes.

"I gotta do this, Dad," he said. "This feeling won't set me free, and the only way I know how to get there is to make this right. I hope I'm making the right decision, because I do wanna see you and Mommy again, but I gotta handle this. Tell everyone I said hello."

Franky waited to hear a sign from his father as he walked, but none came. He had no idea where he was going, but he figured he would know when he got there. He walked to Joseph E. Lowery Boulevard and picked up his pace. He walked into the parking lot of the Shell gas station and paused. The police car was where he thought it would be—right in front of the store. The officer inside the car was fiddling around on his computer screen and drinking coffee. Oh, how he hated those guys. Where were they when he and Khadija were getting jumped by a pack of dummies? Yet they were Johnny on the spot when Nigel was doing a good deed.

Franky walked into the store.

"Hey, Franky," Habib, the Arab owner, said. "How you doing, my friend?"

Franky didn't respond. He and Habib had always been on good terms and often shared deep conversations about religion and politics. He walked over to the refrigerator and removed a bottle of Pepsi. He closed the door and walked past Habib and out the door.

"Franky," Habib called. "Franky . . ."

Franky kept walking as if he didn't hear a word the man said. He kept walking until he reached the police car. He stopped and knocked on the window.

The officer looked at him but didn't move.

Franky shook his soda and knocked again.

The officer sighed and shook his head as if he was chalking Franky up to being a pesky teenager.

Franky shook the soft drink a little harder, then knocked again.

"What?" the officer barked through the closed window.

"Maybe you didn't get the memo about serving and protecting," Franky said.

"What?" the officer said as he finally rolled down his window.

Franky opened the top of the Pepsi and sprayed the drink all over the officer's pale face.

The officer jumped back and wasted his coffee all over his paperwork and computer. The man turned beet red and opened his door and jumped out. He glared down at Franky. "Have you lost your mind?"

Habib was outside the store now. He was short, chubby, and wore a black shemagh on his head. "Franky," he said in his heavy Arab accent. "You forgot to pay for that, my friend."

"I stole it," he said.

"No," Habib said as if all hope was lost. "No say that, my friend."

"Oh, yeah," the officer said. "Great. Put your hands behind your back. You are under arrest."

"No," Habib said, shaking his head. "He can have it. He didn't steal it. He's a good boy. Franky, what's wrong?"

Franky didn't respond. His mind was on the task at hand.

"He's going to jail anyway," the officer said.

"Why?" Habib asked. "Give him a break."

The officer paused, pondering doing Habib a favor.

Franky saw the indecision on the officer's face. He couldn't have this man changing his mind, so he lifted his leg and stomped down on the officer's foot as hard as he could.

"That's it. Assault on a police officer," the cop said.

Franky was handcuffed and placed in the back of the police car. He could feel himself slipping into another world.

21

The Atlanta City Jail looked totally different on the inside than it did when Franky visited his cousins on their trips in and out of the place. The city put on a good face for the visiting public, but there was an entirely different world once the police officer pulled into the underground tunnel to the intake area.

Two heavyset armed guards were the welcoming committee, one black and the other white. They didn't smile as they chatted with the arresting officer before walking to the back of the police cruiser. The locks on the back door were popped, and one of the members of the welcoming committee snatched Franky out of the backseat. His hands were still cuffed behind his back, and they lifted his arms up, causing him a great amount of pain. They then literally carried him through two different sets of steel doors. He was dumped on the floor of a large room. The black officer kneeled down, placed his knee on Franky's back, and removed the cuffs. Franky never said a word, and he was mishandled. This was just par for the course. He was searched, and everything he had in his pockets was taken, including Khadija's phone. His personal items were placed in a plastic bag. Franky was handed a black Sharpie and asked to write his name on the bag. He refused. The officer didn't ask twice; he just took the bag, scribbled something on it, and walked away.

Franky stood up and looked around. He was in a room with hundreds of people who were under arrest just like him, and the place smelled awful. Foul-smelling drunks who were talking crazy and threatening to fight the officers stumbled around. About ten prostitutes were sitting on a long bench, and Franky couldn't help but wonder if they were even fifteen years old. A few pimps huddled in a corner trying to steer clear of any trouble. Drug addicts, scratching their arms trying to calm that need for another fix, sat on the floor mumbling to themselves. Then there were the juveniles. They were buck wild and seeking attention in the worst way. Franky wondered why he was being placed in a jail that included grown-ups, but he didn't say anything. His mind was on the task at hand.

He walked over to a long row of chairs and took a seat. Even this miserable environment couldn't take his mind off of Khadija. Franky looked at a bum who was sitting on the floor in the holding area and did a double take—the bum looked like his father. The man was staring directly at him with the same stern face his father used to give him when he did something that he wasn't supposed to. He peered in closer, and the man's face changed. His heart skipped a beat. One of his dad's biggest claims to fame was that he had never seen the inside of a jail cell—quite an accomplishment considering where and how he grew up—and yet it was his son who was sitting in one. He dropped his head.

"Everybody under the age of seventeen line up over here," one of the correction officers said in a booming voice. "If I find anyone in line that is over the age of seventeen, you will have new charges added to what you already have."

A guy in a lime-green outfit—pants, shirt, suit coat, and matching hat—jumped up and walked over to the line. He appeared to be older than the age limit for the line.

"How old are you?" the guard asked.

"Sixteen," the guy said.

"And let me guess. You're a wannabe pimp," the guard said, shaking his head. "You look like a fool."

"He looks like a Laffy Taffy," one of the kids in line said.

The sixteen-year-old pimp turned around and walked toward the boy as if he wanted to fight but was snatched back into line by the guard.

"I'ma see you, boi," Lime Green said, still trying to go after the jokester.

"Everybody can see you," the jokester said, laughing. "And trust me, player. This ain't what you want. Believe that."

"Hey," the guard said. "Y'all are pathetic. This is jail and y'all still up in here acting up. Stand your lil simple-minded self still before I take you in one of those rooms over there and strap you to a wall."

Franky looked where the officer was pointing and saw two people strapped into restraint chairs. Their mouths were gagged, and white mesh bags were on their heads.

Once all of the teens were lined up, they were led to a side door and out of the holding tank. They ended up in a small room with a bunch of desks and computers. About five or six officers sat behind a large counter. The teens were made to stand on a wall and wait to be fingerprinted and have their mug shots taken.

"I want you guys to count from first to last. Go," a corrections officer said.

When it was Franky's turn to count, he didn't say a word.

"Hey," the officer said, running at Franky and screaming at the top of his lungs. "Can you hear? I said count."

Franky turned toward the man, then calmly turned away, keeping his eyes straight ahead.

"Okay," the officer said. "I think we got a deaf one. Keep the count going. The mute here is number twelve."

After the count was completed, all twenty-five juveniles, boys and girls, were fingerprinted and had their mug shots taken.

When Franky stepped up, he looked at the camera with such a menacing face that the lady taking the picture stopped what she was doing and looked at him. "My God, son," she said with a frown. "You're too young and handsome to have that much anger inside of you."

Franky didn't respond, nor did he change his facial expression. The lady shook her head and snapped his picture from the front and side of his face.

The teen prisoners were laughing and joking around as if they were headed off to summer camp, but Franky couldn't even hear them. After the mug shot and the fingerprints, Franky was asked once again to provide his name and date of birth, and once again he refused. The officer put John Doe down on a paper and moved him along. The juvies were led out of the room and outside into a parking garage. They were handcuffed and loaded

onto a white bus with the words GEORGIA DEPARTMENT OF
CORRECTIONS on the side. Franky sat in the front seat, a
good habit that was hard to break. He stared out the window at the city of Atlanta as the bus carried him to a life he
always said he wanted no part of. His mind began to wan-
der as he sat there with his hands cuffed on his lap. He
looked up at a billboard and saw an advertisement for an
Atlanta home builder, and the picture on the sign was of a
house that looked exactly like the one he had shared with
his parents in Jefferson Parish. He kept his eyes on the
sign until it was no longer in his sight and wondered what
God was trying to tell him.

Metro Juvenile Housing Facility was about a thirty-five
minute bus ride from downtown Atlanta, and when they
arrived at the juvenile prison, Franky was surprised at how
big it was. He looked up at the thirty-foot high guard tow-
ers and saw a man staring down at them. The guard had a
rifle across his body and seemed to be ready to use it at
any time. The bus stopped, and the boys and girls were
told to get off. The twenty boys were led into one building
and the five girls were led into another. Once inside, the
boys were told to strip naked. Franky followed the directions that were given to him, and with each new directive,
he felt more humiliated. This was a heavy price to pay for
some revenge, but he was willing to endure. Looking
around at his cocriminals, he could tell that the vast majority of the guys had been incarcerated many times before. Some of them were on cruise control and did things
even before they were asked to do them, but Franky was
in total disgust with this entire experience which made
him even more upset.

As he stood there, as naked as the day he was born, his

anger grew, and he had trouble keeping himself from lashing out at everyone in the room. He was a time bomb waiting to explode, and he could feel himself slipping fast over to the side where kids didn't care if they lived or died. Franky was inspected and then sprayed with some kind of insecticide. He was then given a navy blue jumpsuit, orange flip-flops, a T-shirt, and a pair of underwear. All of his clothes were placed in a brown paper bag. He was then led to a meeting room where an older lady sat behind a desk.

"Have a seat," she said, peering over the top of her glasses.

Franky took a seat.

"Spell your name, first then last," she said.

Franky wrote his name.

"Do you have any allergies, diseases, or thoughts of suicide?"

"No," he said.

"Ever been arrested before?"

"No."

The lady stopped writing and erased what she had assumed would be a yes answer. She looked at Franky for a full thirty seconds without saying anything.

"Can I go now?"

"Not yet," the lady said, turning back to her pad. "Where are you from, Mr. Bourgeois?"

"Nawlins," he said, unintentionally using the slang term for his hometown.

"Me too," she said. "Which part of the city?"

"Third Ward, Calliope Projects," he said, even though he had only visited the place four or five times in his entire life.

"I don't think so, but if you say so," the lady said. "What brings you to Atlanta?"

"Katrina," he said.

The lady nodded. "That storm uprooted a lot of families. Have you notified your parents or guardians of your arrest?"

"Nope."

"Would you like to use the phone to let your mother know where you are?"

"I can't," he said.

"Why not?"

"Because."

The lady looked at Franky again as if staring at him hard and long enough would get some answers from him.

"Why not?" she asked again.

"Because my mother is dead and so is my father."

"Who do you live with?"

"My cousins," he said.

"Would you like to call your cousins?"

"No," he said.

The lady turned to her computer and started typing. She looked over at Franky and gave him a fake smile. "Okay," she said. "It is important for you to know that you have not been convicted of any crime. You are simply being detained until you can see a judge. You will go to court tomorrow or the next, and the judge may decide to send you home, which he probably will, given your lack of history and being that the charge is kind of petty. The officer wrote it up as assault, but I'm sure your attorney will say you just wasted your drink and stepped on his toe by mistake. Whatever the case is, you make sure to keep your nose clean while you're here. So many times guys come in

here with a nothing charge but decide to get into an altercation and end up with some charge that will give him
more time. I'm going to make sure you room with somebody who has a good head on his shoulders—since you
refuse to call anyone to pick you up."

Franky heard the woman, but he didn't hear her. His
mind was still fixated on Tyrone.

"You can step out into the hallway. A guard will take
you where you need to go," the woman said.

Franky stood and walked toward the door.

"Oh," the lady said. "I'm really sorry to hear about your
parents, Mr. Bourgeois."

Franky grabbed the door handle and walked out without so much as a nod to the woman.

The guard led Franky to a cell that was smaller than his
bathroom at home. On the wall was a stainless-steel sink
and toilet combo. When he stepped in, he saw the bottom
bunk bed was empty but there was a boy sleeping on the
top one. Franky walked over and pulled the covers off the
boy's head. He looked directly into the boy's face, and
once he realized that this wasn't his target, he threw the
covers back over him. The boy never moved.

Franky rolled the thin mattress across the steel slab that
was bolted to the wall and spread out his sheets. He sat
down and slid up until his back was against the wall. He
wondered why he wasn't afraid or even nervous about
being incarcerated. This was quite abnormal behavior, he
realized, but before he could get too deep into his thoughts,
the zee monster came and took him away.

22

Nigel woke up and knocked on Franky's bedroom door. "Getcha head out the bed, whoadie," he said, and walked into the kitchen. He was in a good mood, so he decided he would send his cousin to school with a hot breakfast.

"I'm cooking breakfast, ya heard? Cereal is cool, but every now and then the body needs something hot to start its day," he said to Franky's door.

He walked into the kitchen and pulled out a well-used pot and pan. He opened the refrigerator and removed the eggs and bacon.

"Franky," he called out. "You want French toast or grits?"

No answer.

Nigel shook his head. "For somebody who loves school, you sho don't like to get up and go there. You been out for a week. Now it's time to get back in the swing of things, ya heard?"

Nigel measured some water, poured it into the pot, and

once it began to boil, he added the grits. The bacon was thin, and it was going to take cooking the entire pack just to satisfy Franky's teenage hunger. He walked over to the refrigerator and checked to see if Rico had killed all of the orange juice like he normally did. Yep, it was all gone. Speaking of Rico, he had been missing in action for the last two days. Once Stick was flushed out, he started spending a lot of time with that weird-looking geechie woman and hadn't been coming home or calling. Nigel wasn't really all that concerned, because the woman proved to be good for him. When Rico was all set to shoot up the entire city after Franky got jumped, the geechie woman put her hand on his shoulders, and he calmed down immediately and never mentioned it again. It was as if the woman had some kind of hold over him. But, after all, she was a geechie woman. Nigel wished he had her around a long time ago. He picked up the house phone and dialed his brother's cell.

"What's cracka lacking?" Rico's sleepy voice said.

"That woman must've put a root on you, too," Nigel said.

"She don't do no roots, man," Rico said. "What's up?"

"My bad, whoadie. A little touchy there, huh?"

Rico only exhaled.

"I guess you forgot that you live here?" Nigel said.

"Nah," Rico said. "I've just been hanging, ya know. Vibing with Donita. She's only nineteen years old, man. I thought she was older."

"You're only eighteen," Nigel said.

"I know that, but I just thought she was older."

"So when is she gonna come around? I only saw her that one time last week when you wanted to shoot up the city."

"Man," Rico said, "gone wit dat. I'm done with all that violence. 'Bout to go back to school, too. Get my GED."

"Did I dial the wrong number? Is this Rico Bourgeois?"

"Live and direct. I'm just saying. We been talkin', ya know. Talkin' 'bout life. The future, ya know."

"I ain't mad atcha," Nigel said. "First of all, she sets me free, and now she's about to do the same thing for you."

"I'm already free, whoadie."

"If you say so," Nigel said.

"We went to the movies last night, and I'm telling you this girl got some serious powers for real, man. I had to go sit somewhere else because she kept telling me what was gonna happen. She ain't even seen the doggone thang before but know everything 'bout it. That's crazy."

"Yeah, okay," Nigel said. "Hey, who am I to say any different? I'm home with all the charges dropped, Stick is locked up, and you're going back to school. The world is a lovely place."

"That's what I'm talking 'bout," Rico said. "And you won't believe where she found this fool at. Some lil small town in south Georgia. Fool was on a farm sleeping in a cow pasture."

"How she find him out there? Never mind. She's the geechie woman. Nuff said," Nigel said, laughing as he flipped the bacon. "That's a'ight. Money well spent."

"And guess what else?"

"What?" Nigel said.

"Guess who I bumped into at the movies last night?"

"Why do I have to guess? Why can't you just tell me?"

"Kelli," Rico said.

"Our aunt Kelli?"

"Yep, mean old Kelli. She came up to me and pinched

me on the ear. I'm waiting in line to get some popcorn and somebody pinched me so hard I almost turned around and stole on her, ya heard?"

"Oh, yeah," Nigel said. "And she would've stole on you right back."

"I know. Soon as I realized it was her, I got scared. That girl used to terrorize me when I was little."

"Did you get her number?"

"Yeah, I got it. You got something to write with?"

"Yeah," Nigel said. "Even though she didn't like us too much when we was growing up, she's still family."

"I know," Rico said. "She asked about you. But, man, she was going crazy when I told her Franky was with us. She started crying and everything. Said she'd been calling the schools, hospitals, the jails. I told her he ain't been to none of them," Rico said with a chuckle as he gave his brother the number.

"Okay," Nigel said. "I'll call her as soon as I get this boy up and at 'em. You know he'll sleep his life away if you let him."

"He's pregnant," Rico said.

"Must be. And I like how you killed all of the orange juice."

"Franky must've did that this time 'cause I ain't been there."

"Yeah. Well, I need to run down to the store and get some."

"A'ight, man. I'll probably be back over there today. I need to talk to you."

"About what?" Nigel asked. "What's wrong?"

"I swear you're a worry wart. Nothing is wrong. It's just I'm thinking 'bout moving back down to Nawlins."

"You moving back to Nawlins or you going out to the swamp with the geechie girl?"

"Nawlins, man," Rico said. "I told you I'm going back to school. Ain't no schools in the swamps."

"Yeah, okay. You're grown now, so it's whatever you wanna do. We still got our people there. You'll be okay."

"You for real," Rico said.

"Yeah, whoadie," Nigel said. "If that's whatchu wanna do, then that's what you need to do. I wanna move back myself, but I don't think Franky needs to be down there right now, ya heard."

"Yeah," Rico said. "A'ight. I need to get back to cuddling up with my silver-haired stunner."

"Peace," Nigel said, and hung up the phone.

He turned off his bacon and placed it on a napkin-layered plate. He looked at the clock and realized he had time to drive to the corner store to pick up some orange juice and still get Franky up. He turned off the stove and walked back toward Franky's room.

"Franky," he called again, knocking on the door. "I'ma run to the store right quick. I'll be back in five minutes. You better be up and at 'em or I'ma come in there and throw some water on ya."

Nigel walked away from the door and out of the house. He jumped in his car and was down at the store in less than two minutes. He jumped out of his car, looked at the police officer who was parked directly out in front of the store, and ignored him.

"Habib," Nigel said. "Good morning, homie."

"Hey," Habib said as if he was waiting on Nigel to show up. "What in the goodness is going on with your cousin?"

"Huh?"

"He came in my store and stole from me. That's not nice," Habib said.

"Stole from you?"

"Yes," Habib said. "Did I stutter? Stole from me. Your ears are working just fine."

"What do you mean he stole from you? Stole what?"

"I've been very kind to you and your family. I let you have things and pay me later. Do I not?"

"Yes, and we always pay you for them, too," Nigel said defensively. "Do we not?"

"Well, Franky came in here last night and was acting really weird. He didn't even speak. That's not like him. That's what always separated him from these knuckleheads around here. He's cultured. But last night, he came in here and walked out with a Pepsi without paying me. Didn't even say a thing," Habib said, shaking his head.

"But Franky don't steal," Nigel said.

"That's what I thought, but he came in here last night and stole. Surprised me, too," Habib said.

"Really," Nigel said, reaching into his pocket to pay for the stolen good. "How much do I owe you for the Pepsi he took?"

"Nothing," Habib said, fanning him off. "You just tell him to come and apologize. And I want him to explain to me what was wrong him. He's my friend and I'm concerned."

"I will," Nigel said, deep in thought.

"Then," Habib said, jumping up as if he just remembered something else, "guess what else he did? He poured the Pepsi on the police officer. Didn't even drink it. They locked him up."

"What?"

"Yes, I pleaded with the officer but he paid me no mind."

"Who locked him up?"

"The officer who parks here every night. The big-eared white boy. He still may be outside. But they took my friend to jail," Habib said, shaking his head. "It was almost like he wanted to go. The officer was gonna let him go after I said good things about him, but when the guy seemed like he was gonna let him go, Franky hauled off and kicked him. Kicked him good, too. Strange. I tell you, very strange."

Nigel reached into his pocket and slid a five-dollar bill under the bulletproof window that separated Habib from the customers who frequented his store.

"No," Habib protested. "I can't take that."

"Yes, you can," Nigel said, and ran outside. The police officer was pulling off just as Nigel made it outside.

"Hey!" he called out, but the officer was already on Martin Luther King Boulevard and speeding down the street. "Daggone it," he said, punching his own hand in frustration.

Nigel jumped into his car and raced back up the block to his house. He pulled into the driveway, jumped out of the car, and started running. He ran inside the house and straight back to Franky's room. He opened the door and looked inside, hoping that Habib had just had a bad dream. Franky wasn't anywhere to be found. Nigel growled in frustration and ran around the house, looking for his cousin. He sighed and look around as if Habib and Franky had got together to film an episode of *Punk'd*. But his life was far from a television show. Looking around his cousin's room, he knew that Franky was exactly where Habib said he was.

The phone rang and he rushed out of the room to get it, hoping it was Franky.

"Hello?" he said.

"May I speak to Franky?" a girl's voice said.

"He's not here," Nigel said. "Who is calling?"

"This is Khadija," she said. "Will you tell him I called?"

"Oh, how you doing, Khadija?" Nigel said. "I didn't recognize your voice."

"I'm doing okay. I was trying to catch Franky before he left for school."

"You already missed him. I haven't heard from you in a few days. You doing okay?"

"Yes," Khadija said. "I'm okay. Will you tell Franky to call me? I really need to talk to him."

"I'll do it," Nigel said.

"Okay," Khadija said. "Please don't forget to tell him that I called."

"I won't," Nigel said before hanging up.

Nigel walked back to Franky's door and stared at his empty bed. His heart was heavy, and he felt responsible for where Franky was, because he didn't press him hard enough for answers when he started acting weird after he got jumped. His interest in school dropped, he never went to meet the football coach, and he stayed in his room staring at the wall. Now that his little cousin had finally snapped, he couldn't help but take the blame.

Nigel saw Auntie Kelli's telephone number, picked the phone up, and dialed it. He had done the best he could for Franky and he'd failed. It was time for someone else to try.

23

A loud horn sounded, and Franky slowly opened his eyes. He looked around and tried to figure out where he was. He was still sitting upright with his back against the wall. A set of feet plopped down in front of his face, followed by a body. A person jumped from the top bunk and turned around to look at him.

"What's up?" the guy said.

Franky didn't respond. He ignored the brown-skinned guy with tattoos on his face. There was a black tattoo of a cross between his eyes and two teardrops on the outside of his left eye.

"It's breakfast time," the boy said. "And you gotta get up and eat."

The boy was about Franky's height but was heavier. Franky sized him up and figured he should be on somebody's football field instead of in the county's jail cell, but then again so should he. He stood up and stretched.

"I'm DeMarco. People call me Dee," he said, reaching out his hand.

Franky gave his hand a halfhearted slap.

"What's your name, homie?" Dee asked.

"Franky," he said. "Do you know a guy in here named Tyrone?"

"Black Tyrone?"

"He's black," Franky said.

"It's two of them in here. One is light skinned and the other one is as black as a car tire. The light-skin one is cool, but Black Ty is a buster. He just got here a few days ago. Loudmouth with a missing front tooth? I guess somebody got tired of that big mouth and fired him up."

"How can I get at him?" Franky asked, excited at the opportunity. "He's gotta pay for some things he did."

"Well, you will see him in a few minutes. We all eat together," Dee said, smiling in anticipation of some action.

"What about the guards? I only need a few minutes with him," Franky said, licking his lips.

"A few minutes ain't happening, bro, but you can get to him. There is no such thing as a long fight in here. Guards are on their jobs. I've been in here so many times that I know their steps in my sleep. I'll tell you when you'll have more time, but it won't be at breakfast."

"So when?"

"Classrooms are always good," he said. "But you will still get only a minute or so at most. Me and a few of my people can stand in the way and give you a lil more time, but the thing is, they gonna send us back to our rooms for the rest of the day and that's gonna cost you."

"What's it gonna cost me?"

Dee shrugged his shoulders. "Not much. Nobody likes him. He talks too much and he's fugazy."

"What's that?" Franky asked.

"Fake."

"Count time. Line up," a voice said from out in the corridor.

"Let's go, cuz," Dee said. "The hacks get to trippin' if we don't get out here before they come to do their lil count."

Room, Franky took note of how calm and at home Dee seemed. He wasn't trying to get too comfortable in this place. But he was willing to stay as long as he could to make Tyrone pay for his cowardly act. Yet Franky knew that if he carried out the plans that were dancing around in his head, he, too, would have to get comfortable with that thin mattress and the steel doors.

They stepped out of their room and stood by the door. The first floor was for no violent offenders and those who could be bailed out at any time. The second floor was where you could find all of the head cases and career juvenile offenders. Franky looked up and was amazed at the size of the place. There had to be at least one hundred rooms, and two kids were standing by each one. The place looked like it was right out of the movie *Lockdown.* Everywhere he looked, he saw nothing but steel and glass. There was a control room directly in front of him that opened and closed doors, called for more officers if there was a riot, and watched the juvenile delinquents' every move.

Once the corrections officer was satisfied that everyone was accounted for, he asked them to turn to their right, place their hands behind their backs, and march to the mess hall.

Franky scanned every face he saw, trying to find Tyrone, but he didn't see him. Every kid had on the same navy blue jumpsuit with the exception of a few sprinkled around who wore orange ones.

"Why do they have on orange?" Franky asked Dee as they walked.

"They got big charges," Dee said. "Or they're about to turn eighteen, and if that's the case, they are out of here and about to go over to the adult spot. I ain't ever tryna go there, bro."

"Me neither," Franky said. "I'm tryna make this my one and only stop, ya heard."

"You from New Orleans, huh?"

"Yeah."

"Ya the only ones who say 'ya heard' fifty times a sentence. 'Ya heard,' " Dee said. "Yeah, I heard ya. I'm standing right here."

Franky kept looking for Tyrone as they walked. They made it to the mess hall, and Franky slowly trudged up and got his tray. The place was surprisingly quiet. Franky placed his tray in front of the old lady who was waiting to serve the juvies. She slapped a big wad of some funky-looking white mixture onto his plate and jerked her finger to the right, signaling for him to keep moving. The next server gave him some boiled eggs, and the next guy gave him burned toast. He grabbed a carton of milk from a stainless-steel tub and walked over to an empty table by the wall. He didn't touch his food; his attention was on the faces of the guys coming into the mess hall.

There he was.

Franky stood up, but before he could take a step toward his enemy, Dee blocked his path.

"You can't do it right here, cuz," Dee said. "The most you gonna get is a punch in, and they will keep y'all separated forever. So sit tight. Come sit with us."

"Well, looky-looky here," Tyrone said. "How ya doing, New Orleans? Or should I say, how's Khadija?"

Franky stood up, but Dee's large hand grabbed his shoulder and slammed him back down.

"Ignore him for now. He knows nothing is jumping off in here."

"See that fool," Tyrone said to one of the guys who was standing by him. "That's why I'm locked up. Crushed that fool and I knocked his lil stink girlfriend out, too. One punch, boi. Bam! Right in her ugly face."

The boys with Tyrone stared at him—so did everyone else in earshot of the loudmouth.

Franky was boiling inside. His eyes began to water because he wanted to go after Tyrone so bad.

"You crying, man?" one of the guys at his table asked.

"Nah," Dee said. "He ain't crying. That's pain. Loudmouth is in trouble."

"Whatchu do to get up in here, New Orleans?" Tyrone asked as he went to another area of the mess hall. "Stole a schoolbook? Ya nerd. I'ma see ya around, boi."

Franky dropped his head and massaged his temples. Seeing the guy who had turned his world upside down and not be able to touch him was pure torture.

"Let him talk. Dig his own grave," Dee said.

Franky stood and walked over to his table to get his tray. He noticed that someone had taken his milk. "Who took my milk?" he barked.

The guys at the table next to him snickered and laughed among themselves. Franky walked over and saw one guy with his hand behind his back. He stared down at the boy. "You got three seconds to give me that milk back."

The boy looked at his friends with a smirk on his face, but Franky could see the fear in his eyes.

"One," Franky said. "Two."

"Give it up," Dee said.

The boy's smirk disappeared and without a word handed Franky the carton.

Franky reached out and snatched it out of his hand. He glared at the boy, who only looked down at his plate.

"So what's your beef with Loudmouth?" Dee asked. "Oh, hold up. This is Zimir and that's Detric," he said, pointing at a guy who was so big he was almost bursting out of his jumpsuit and at a small guy who looked to be about ten years old.

"He and a few of his friends jumped me and my girl. He hit her in the face with a roll of quarters and put her in the hospital."

"Why'd he do that?" Detric, the small guy, asked.

"He came up to me at school talking about how some dudes from Nawlins shot his potna, and I guess he blamed me. So I punched him in the face and knocked him and his tooth out. He's a clown. So he got his lil coward friends to attack me and my girl. Now my girl's parents moved her away and she's not talking to me."

"Sounds like he needs a whipping," Zimir said. "My daddy is from New Orleans. I used to go down there every summer. I wanna hit up that Mardi Gras, though. I bet it be some honeys down there."

Franky nodded, but his eyes were on Tyrone, who was laughing and joking around like he didn't have a care in the world. If he only knew.

"Where do we go after we leave here?" Franky asked, plotting how to get at Tyrone.

"After here, we go to class. Kind of relaxed over there. You can have at him for a good fifty, maybe sixty seconds before somebody come running. Then if you ain't happy with your handiwork, we can block the guards for a few more seconds, but if we get in trouble, that's gonna cost you a few honey buns."

"I had some money on me when I got here. Will they let me buy stuff with that?" Franky asked.

"Yeah," Dee said.

"Honey buns," Zimir said, licking his lips. "I'ma need to get about three of those."

The same horn that woke Franky up sounded again, and everyone jumped up to empty their trays. They were lined up again in single file, then walked with their hands behind their backs until they made it to the school.

"What's up, Mr. Banks?" Dee said to a tall bald-headed guy who looked to be in his late thirties or early forties. "When you gonna bring me a new book?"

"As soon as you learn how to speak proper English. Besides, you haven't read the last one I gave you," Mr. Banks said.

"Yes, I did," Dee said. "*Black Boy* by Richard Wright? Come on, man. I been read that."

"Okay," Mr. Banks said. "We'll be discussing it at book club tonight. I hope you're telling the truth, because if you're lying, I'm kicking you out of the club for a week."

"When have you ever known me to lie?" Dee said.

"Ah," Mr. Banks said, scratching his head. "Every time you open your mouth."

"Stop flexing," Dee said. "You know my word is my bond. Never met anybody I cared enough about to lie. I don't care what nobody think, so why would I lie?"

"Y'all got a book club in here?" Franky asked.

"Yeah," Dee said. "Mr. Banks is a writer—he has like ten books out. He started the book club in here, donated a bunch of books to the library and everything. Before he did that, we had all these books donated by white churches and stuff. *Gone with the Wind* and stuff like that. Man, I need to read some Jihad, Eric Jerome Dickey, some Shannon Holmes or something."

"That's what's up," Franky said.

"Yeah, Mr. Banks is a real dude. He said if I stay out of trouble, he'll pay for me to go to college. Ain't that crazy? My own daddy never told me that, and he has big money. Mr. Banks is the first man I ever met who's ever took the time to teach me anything. That's real talk right there, player," Dee said.

"How much longer you got in here?"

"About three more and then I'm out," Dee said. "I got a lil petty theft charge, but it's like my tenth offense, so the judge gave me six months. Bad thing about it is I'll be back. I've been locked up thirty something times, bro."

Franky felt sorry for him because he seemed like such a cool guy. If he only had a little guidance, there was no telling what he could be.

"You can stay out if you want to, man," Franky said.

"That's what Mr. Banks says, but I'll be leaving here going right back to my hood. And trust me when I tell you that ain't nuttin' there but trouble. I live in the Bluff. You ever heard of it?"

Franky had heard about the Bluff, and it was rough. Lots of bad things happened over there because the people lived far below the poverty level.

"You said your dad has big dough," Franky asked. "Why y'all live in the Bluff?"

"Because that fool don't want nothing to do with me or my sister. I hear he's one of these NBA dudes. That's what my grandma told me, but it don't matter. He ain't ever spent one second of his time with us, so forget him."

"Maybe you can see if Mr. Banks is as real as you think he is. Tell him you don't wanna go back over there and see if he can help you," Franky said.

"Yeah," Dee said as if he had never thought of that. "I'ma do that. I'm tired of coming to jail, but crazy as it sounds, it's better in here than it is at my house. At least in here I get three hots and a cot. At home, it's everybody for themselves."

"Yeah," Franky said, because he certainly could relate.

They walked into the class, where an old white woman sat at her desk. She had to be at least seventy-five years old, and Franky wondered what she would do to defend herself if one of the kids tried to do something. He got his answer when a mammoth-sized security officer, stepped into the class.

"Man," Franky said, looking up to the guy.

"That's Scales. He's cool," Dee said. "Nuttin' but a big old teddy bear."

The boys filed into the classroom and took their seats. As soon as Franky sat down, he saw someone come running at him. He jumped up just as Tyrone's fist came flying at him. He dodged his nemesis and pushed his back so that Tyrone's momentum sent him flying face-first into the cinder-block wall. There was a loud thud, and Franky was on him. He turned the boy around so that he was facing him and punched him as hard as he could in the face. Tyrone's face frowned up from the impact of the punch. Franky hit him again and again and again. Tyrone staggered but raised his hands into a southpaw stance and threw a weak jab that missed Franky by a mile. Franky sidestepped him and landed another punch to Tyrone's jaw that dropped him. Franky pounced on him, straddling his chest and hitting him with every ounce of strength he had. He punched Tyrone for every wrong that ever came his way. Tyrone's face was the target for all the pain and anguish he'd felt since his family was destroyed. He hit him for Khadija and for ruining the most precious friendship he'd ever had. Then he grabbed both Tyrone's ears and lifted his head off the ground to bang it on the hard tile floor.

"Franky," Franky Sr. said in a very calm voice.

Franky looked up and saw his father standing over him. He wasn't there as some ghost or vision; he was really there. He had on the same clothes, and his shoes were still glowing. He paused and looked at his father.

"Do you think you've proved your point?"

No, Dad, Franky thought. *He gotta pay. Do you know what he did?*

"Of course I know what he did. He'll be in jail for the next three years for it. So what else do you want?"

"I want his life," Franky whispered out loud.

"That's not smart."

"Maybe I'm just not smart anymore."

"Franky, my son. If you hit that boy's head on that floor, he will have permanent brain damage. He won't

have any memory of his incarceration. Therefore, he won't really be punished for what he did."

"I don't care what he has," Franky said.

"Yes, you do. You don't care now because you are angry at the world, but you are a good person."

"I used to be."

"You still are, but if you slam his head on that floor, you will never see us again nor will we be able to see you. There is a price to pay for your actions. There is life after this, Franky. But if you slam his head on that floor, you will spend the rest of your life as a street person who never maximized his potential. You will always be in and out of prison and never find happiness. The choice is yours. You're at the crossroads."

Franky still had Tyron's head in his hands. His anger had a stranglehold on him as he lifted the boy's head high, growled, and with all of his force slammed Tyrone's head down. But the head wouldn't hit the floor. It landed softly on the glowing shoes his father was wearing.

Franky looked up into the eyes of his father. Franky Sr. looked at his son, shook his head in disappointment, and vanished.

24

Franky sat alone in his room. He had his back against the wall with his arms hugging his knees. He couldn't shake seeing the look of disappointment on his dad's face. Now he was really feeling bad and couldn't believe how foolish he was for allowing his anger to consume him like that. But was that really his dad or had he been hallucinating? He seemed so real, but why now? After all of these years, why was he showing up now? These questions racked his brain as his door to his room swung open.

"Good Lord, cuz," Dee said. "You're an animal. That boy had to be shipped out to the emergency room. Serves the loudmouth right, though."

Franky exhaled and looked straight ahead.

"But get this," Dee said. "The only thing they're gonna do to you is send you to cool down because everybody saw him attack you. It's self-defense, cuz. And old big Scales didn't like him either—you see him taking his time coming over there to pull you off of him?"

Franky didn't respond. His mind was still on his dad.

"I still need to get my honey bun because I threw in an extra lie and said he came at you with a pencil," Dee said. "That made it sound a little better. Plus, it added to his charge and made it aggravated."

Franky finally looked up at his roommate, then around the room and took a deep breath. He stood up and started pacing back and forth without saying anything.

Dee stepped back and stared at Franky like something was wrong with him.

"I need to get out of here," Franky said now that he had taken care of what he had come here to do.

Dee relaxed and propped his leg up on the stainless-steel toilet seat. He had seen this many times before in his numerous stays in juvie hall. Some folks could go days before they realized that they were trapped and then snap, then there were some who crack right away. But everybody snapped at some point.

A guard appeared at the door and gave Franky a menacing look. "Bourgeois?" he asked, looking at a clipboard.

"Yes," Franky said.

"Look here," the guard said. "We have you down here as not having made your phone call. What's your problem? Do you have anybody you can call? Because they can come and sign you out. If you don't, we're calling DFCS."

That was all he had to say. He didn't want any part of the Division of Family and Children Services.

"I can call my family," Franky said.

"Good," the guard said, shaking his head. "I don't know what's wrong with you young boys. If I was locked up, I would be running to a phone so somebody could come and get me. Not y'all. Y'all think this is Six Flags or something."

Franky listened without responding. He couldn't care less about too much of anything right now.

"You need to make a phone call before six o'clock this evening, or I'm putting you down as a runaway and calling DFCS. Anybody around here will let you use the phone, and make sure they document it," the guard said, walking off.

"Who can I ask to make a phone call?" Franky asked Jay.

"Well, normally all you had to do was ask to use the phone, but since you're in what they call 'cool down,' you can't leave the room until tomorrow. Twenty-four hours, bro. And that's from the time you get busted, but since he just came up here trippin', I guess you can catch one of the guards around here."

"I gotta stay in this room for twenty-four hours?"

"Yep," Dee said. "Unless your people come and get you. Then you can go home. We need to exchange numbers, man. You good peoples."

"Yeah, we can do that."

"Cool. You don't seem like a street dude, but you fight like one," Dee said, then pulled up his sleeve, displaying an arm full of tattoos.

"I'm not a street dude, and I don't like fighting, but I had to get him. He crossed the line," Franky said.

"Well, you got him."

"How many tattoos do you have, whoadie?"

"I don't know. I lost count a long time ago. I got my first one when I was twelve. I started doing them myself at thirteen. You want one? I'm the best in the business, bro. And I will let you pay me later."

"Nah," Franky said. "I don't do tattoos."

"Why not? Take a look at my work," Dee said, walking over to a stack of books and tablets that were piled on the steel desk. He handed a tablet to Franky. "I can draw anything, but those are some originals I came up with. When I get some money, I'ma start me my own tat shop and call it Dee-toos."

"How do you do tattoos in here?"

"Where there is a will there is a way, brother man. I got all the needles you need to get the job done. They're not electric like the ones I'ma have when I open up Dee-toos, but they're clean and sanitary." Dee opened a little case that was about the size of a pencil box.

"How did you get all that stuff?"

"Man," Dee said with a smile, "I've been coming in here since I was eleven years old. The guards are like my big brothers, so they hook me up. Plus, I give them a cut of the money I make, so they bring me what I need."

Franky flipped through the pages and had to admit, Dee had some major skills. He could draw a picture of a person that looked just like a Kodak shot. The more he flipped through the pages, the more he started to change his mind. Ten minutes later, he had changed his mind and was sitting on the edge of his bed while Dee used his arm as a canvas. Forty-five minutes later, Franky had a tattoo that covered most of his skinny arm.

"This is nice," Franky said once Dee had finished. He looked at his arm in the mirror, which was really a steel slab hanging over the toilet and sink combo, and couldn't help but smile.

"You need to use the phone, bro. Old boy wasn't play-

ing; these folks will have you sitting in a group home before you know it," Dee said as he put away his supplies.

"Yeah," Franky said, still admiring the fantastic-looking
crossbones and New Orleans Saints emblem.

"There's Mr. Banks. He'll let you use his cell. Mr. Banks,"
he called out.

"What's up?" Mr. Banks said, walking over to their room.
"What can I do you gentleman out of?"

"My man here needs to use your phone," Dee said,
nodding at Franky. "Officer Hammond said they're about
to call DFCS on him. Ain't tryna see the homie up in some
group home."

"Does your homie have a name?"

"His name is Franky," Dee said with a wide smile.

"Well, what did I tell you about introducing people like
that?" Mr. Banks asked.

"Franky, this is Mr. Banks. Mr. Banks, this is Franky," Dee
said.

"Very proper, DeMarco," Mr. Banks said, nodding. "You've
come a long way from 'dis my potna nem,' and 'ya know
wha I'm saying shorty, doe.' "

"Aww, man," Dee said, showing a room-brightening
smile. "You know you understood everything I said. You
know you're hood, too."

"Correction, my tattoo-faced friend. I'm from the hood,
but make no mistake about it—there is nothing hood
about me," Mr. Banks said. "Is this the young man who
was fighting?"

"Yep," Dee said, shadow boxing. "He's a beast. You
know I don't roll with no lames. Gotta be able to get down
with the get-down if you gonna be on my team, homie."

"Bye, DeMarco," Mr. Banks said as he walked into the room. "Go hang out in the dayroom for a minute."

"No problem," Dee said. "You homie, he's cool. You can keep it real with him."

Mr. Banks handed Franky his cell phone.

"Thanks," Franky said.

"I'll be right outside the door. Parents or legal guardians only. No girlfriends or homies. Ya dig?"

"Yes, sir," Franky said as he dialed his home number.

"Hello?" Nigel said.

"Hey, Nigel," Franky said.

"Boy," Nigel snapped, "you know I'm gonna choke you, don't you? What's wrong with you? Why are you stealing and pouring soda pops on police officers? Are you crazy? Were you trying to go to jail? Huh?"

"Nigel," Franky said. "Will you calm down?"

"No. I'm not calming down," Nigel said. "Where are you?"

"I'm at a place called Metro. I had to call you or they were going to call DFCS."

"What do you mean, you had to call me? Why didn't you want to call me?"

"I don't know," Franky said.

"You don't know? Franky, have you lost yo mind?"

"I don't know."

Franky could hear his cousin sigh in frustration.

"Well, now that I know where you at, I can speed up the process, ya hear," Nigel said. "Did you tell them folks at the county jail that your name was John Doe?"

"I didn't tell them nothing," Franky said.

"I swear to you I'm gonna put my hands on you, whoadie."

"A'ight," Franky said. "I'm using the counselor's phone, so I gotta go."

"Hey, yo, Franky," Nigel said quickly before Franky hung up. "You okay?"

"Yeah," he said.

"I love ya, whoadie. I don't know where I went wrong or what I did, but I tried to do right by you, ya heard."

"I know. Nothing is your fault. You're good."

"Okay," Nigel said. "I'ma try to get you up outta there today."

"Thanks, Nigel," Franky said.

"I love ya, whoadie."

"Yeah. Same here."

"Hang in there, whoadie," Nigel said.

Franky hung up the phone and handed it back to Mr. Banks.

"What was the fight about?"

"He just came at me. I don't know why. I was defending myself," Franky said.

"So I heard," Mr. Banks said. "Do you have someone coming to pick you up?"

"I think so."

"That's good," Mr. Banks said, reaching in his pocket and coming out with a business card. "Here ya go. You seem to be an okay guy. Call me once you get out of here and we can talk. Maybe I can help you, or maybe you can help me. I run a nonprofit organization, and I might be able to do some things for ya."

"Thanks," Franky said, taking the card.

"Okay," Mr. Banks said, walking over to a stack of books on the floor in the corner. He leaned down and picked them up. "How can anybody else read if this clown has all the books in his room?"

"I guess he likes to read," Franky said.

"Yeah, when he's locked up but when he's home, you can't get him to read a stop sign," Mr. Banks said, walking over to the door with about ten hardcover novels in his arms. "Nice talking with you, Franky. I hope this place will not become a second home for you."

Franky watched the man leave. He stood up and walked over to the door and looked through the glass at all of the kids milling around the dayroom. He slid his hands in his pockets and tried to figure out what he was going to do with his life. He missed Khadija, and he missed his parents, but he couldn't do anything about that. Loving people was a hurtful thing because somehow they always left him. His mind drifted back to the look of disappointment he saw on his dad's face, and he wondered if he would ever see him again.

25

Kelli Bourgeois was a no-nonsense type of girl. She had grown up in the gritty Magnolia Projects, home to rap artist and entrepreneur Master P. Her father had a few kids sprinkled throughout the various wards of New Orleans, but he always took time for her. He would even take around his wife and other kids. She was so much younger than all of her siblings that most people thought she was their child instead of their little sister.

Franky's dad always made time to go and visit her even when the two wards were fighting some kind of senseless war. Franky Sr. always treated Kelli well, and once he got married and started doing well for himself, he made sure she had the best of everything, even going so far as paying for her to study abroad her senior year of high school. That trip to South Africa broadened her horizons and made her realize that as bad as life was in the Magnolia, they lived like kings and queens compared to some of the

people living in huts in parts of South Africa. Once she re-
turned to U.S. soil, she had little patience for slackers.

Kelli was five feet two inches tall and had hazel eyes and
skin the color of honey. She had an easy smile and was always pleasant but professional. Men never approached
her because they said she always looked so mean. She pre-
ferred *focused*. A year before Hurricane Katrina devastated
the region, she had been a student at Xavier University,
but after the storms, she decided to move to Atlanta and
attend Georgia State University.

"Look at you," she said with a wide smile as Franky
walked out into the waiting room of the Metro Juvenile
Housing Facility.

"Hi, Aunt Kelli," Franky said, surprised to see the woman
who looked like a female version of his father.

"How are you doing, boy?" she said, reaching up and
giving her nephew a long hug. "I missed you."

"I'm okay."

"Well, smile, then. Jesus Christ, you look like some kind
of hardened criminal. I haven't seen you in years, and all I
get is a mean ol' face. You've gotten so tall. Oh my goodness," Kelli rattled off.

Franky gave a halfhearted smile.

"Okay," Kelli said, turning around and walking toward
the door. "I know you're ready to get out of here, so let's
go. I've signed all of the paperwork, but you have to come
back to court in about six weeks—that is if I can't get an attorney and speed things up. I'll see what I can do."

Franky nodded. He was really hoping to see Nigel or
even Rico. Even though he hadn't seen his aunt in almost
four years, he always thought of her as being very no-
nonsense and a bit standoffish.

"Where's Nigel?" he asked.

"He's at home. He asked me to come get you," Kelli said, reading his disappointment. "Why the long face?"

Franky shrugged.

"I can ask them to keep you in here for a little while longer if you don't want to come with me," she said with a smile.

"No thank you," Franky said, finally smiling.

"That's what I thought. Are you hungry?"

"Yes," Franky said. "They feed you slop in here that I wouldn't give to a pig."

"Well, it is jail. I don't think those places are supposed to be all that comfortable. What is that on your arm?"

"It's a tattoo," Franky said, displaying Dee's handiwork. "My roommate did it."

"Boy," Kelli said. "You haven't been in that place for a full day and you already have a prison tattoo?"

"It's not prison," Franky said. "It's a youth facility, and they don't have cells, they have rooms."

"I see bars, I see razor-wire fences, and I see guns and men who are ready to use them. Looks like a prison to me," Kelli said, handing Franky a brown paper bag containing all of his belongings.

"I guess you're right," Franky said as he tore open the bag looking for Khadija's phone. Once he saw it, he snatched it out and turned it on.

They made it to Kelli's car, and Franky got in the passenger seat.

"There is a restaurant over by my house called Pappadeaux. Wanna go? They have some really good food."

"Okay," Franky said, fiddling around with Khadija's phone, but the service was turned off. He was hoping that she would get a message to him somehow.

The drive to Pappadeaux took about thirty minutes, and Kelli explained to him how she had been searching high and low for him since the storms. She explained how his father saved her life by swimming through the deep waters to get her and carrying her on his back to safety. She told him that his father's last words to her were to take care of his son.

"Every single day for three years I called every school, hospital, and jail looking for you. Folks back home told me y'all were here, but I didn't know where. I couldn't find you guys," Kelli said on the verge of tears.

"It's okay, Aunt Kelli," Franky said.

"I don't know why those boys didn't make you go to school," she said, shaking her head. "Nigel is just as sweet as can be, but school has never been a priority to him, so I guess he just let you do whatever. But we'll move forward."

Franky knew what that meant. It meant his days with Nigel and Rico just ended.

"So I guess I'll be staying with you now," Franky said, just to confirm his thoughts.

"Oh, yes," she said, nodding. "Definitely! We have to get you back on track. This jail stuff and not going to school isn't going to work."

"I go to school."

"That's not what Rico told me."

"I just started a few weeks ago."

"I see," she said. "Well, we'll figure everything out."

"Where do you live?"

"In Tucker," she said. "Do you know anything about the area?"

"Not really. I heard about a teen club out there."

"Yeah. I think teen clubs are a bad idea. The kids are too undisciplined. They have more shootings at them than the adult ones. So needless to say, you won't be frequenting any of those establishments."

Franky nodded. He was already experiencing another culture shock. Living with his parents, then living with Nigel and Rico, being incarcerated, and now moving in with Kelli. He had a feeling that living with Kelli would be the worst of them all.

"This place is pretty good," she said, turning into the parking lot. "It's not authentic Cajun, but it's a pretty good substitute."

Franky and Kelli walked into the restaurant and waited to be seated. Franky looked around and realized this was the first time he had eaten in a sit-down restaurant since his dad had passed away. The hostess called their name and they were seated. Franky ate like a starving man while Kelli watched and wondered what happened to her sweet little nephew. She could see that his innocence was a thing of the past, but she held on to the fact that she knew his father had taught him well. Once they finished eating, Kelli paid the bill and left a nice tip. They walked outside, got back into her car, and headed over to Nigel and Rico's house to gather his things.

26

There was a small U-Haul truck in the driveway behind Nigel's car. Kelli pulled up to the curb and they got out.

"So this is where you guys are living?" she said, shaking her head. "This is only twenty minutes from me."

They walked up to the house just as Rico was walking out carrying a box.

"Well, if it ain't the jailbird, Franky," Rico said, smiling.

"What's up, Rico?" Franky said. "Where you going?"

"Back to the N.O., whoadie. I had about enough of Atlanta, ya heard?"

"For real," Franky said.

"Yep," Rico said as he walked over and loaded the box into the back of the U-Haul. "How you doing, Kelli?"

"I'm doing just fine, Rico. How are you doing?"

"I'm straight now that I'm headed home."

"I bet you are," she said.

"Whatchu doing with a tattoo, Franky?" Rico asked.

Franky looked down at his arm but didn't say anything.

"It's nice, though, whoadie," Rico said, then walked back into the house.

Franky walked inside the house and noticed that Nigel was placing his clothes into a cardboard box. He stopped packing when he saw his little cousin, and his eyes lit up. "Franky," he said with a wide smile. He dropped his shirt into the box and went over to his cousin and grabbed him. "You okay?"

"Yeah."

Nigel sighed and appeared to be thinking whether he wanted to choke him or hug him. He decided the latter. "I was worried sick 'bout cha, whoadie. I'm glad you okay."

"I'm good," Franky said. He was feeling anxious that the life he had known for the last three years was over without warning. They had had some rough times and lots of hungry nights, but he always felt loved and protected.

"Hi, Kelli," Nigel said, walking over and giving her a hug. "How you doing?"

"I'm good. It's been a long time," she said.

"Yes, it has. I see you've been taking care of yourself. You look good," Nigel said.

"Yeah, but she's still mean," Rico said. "My arm still hurts."

"Come here," she said, motioning with her index finger. "You've gotten a little bigger, but I will still spank your lil tail."

"I know," Rico said before grabbing another box.

Nigel looked down at Franky's arm and frowned. "Where did you get a tattoo from?"

"Jail," Kelli said, shaking her head.

"It's just a tattoo," Franky said.

"Man," Nigel said, disappointment written across his face. "You don't need a tattoo."

"Are you leaving, too?" Franky asked.

"Yeah," Nigel said. "You're gonna go live with Kelli. She's gonna get you back to where you need to be, whoadie. I always told you this street life wasn't for you."

Franky sighed and nodded. He didn't want to go with Kelli. He wanted to stay with his cousins. As dumb and ghetto as they were, they had been all he had for so long.

"I packed up your clothes and stuff already. We gonna try to get on the road tonight. We gotta turn that U-Haul in tomorrow."

Franky nodded and wondered why everybody he loved was leaving him. First his mother, then his dad, then Khadija, and now his cousins. He didn't really know Kelli. She was family, but he didn't really know her, and he feared the unknown.

Rico walked in and looked at Kelli. "Guess what?"

"Chicken butt," she said.

"I'm going back to school," he said, knowing that she would love to hear that.

"That's good, boy. Did you ever finish high school?"

"Nope," Rico said. "Getting my GED and then I'm gonna do a community college."

"Congratulations," Kelli said. "What about you, Nigel?"

"I'm not sure what I'm gonna do, Kelli," he said. "I'm not a school kind of guy, but I'll find my way."

"Yeah," she said. "I'm sure you will."

They all said their good-byes, then loaded Franky's clothes and other personal items into Kelli's car. Franky had to fight back tears as they pulled away from his cousins, who were standing on the front porch waving at him. They were headed back to New Orleans, and he couldn't help but wonder if he would ever see them again.

27

The Village Apartments didn't look anything like the place he had envisioned Kelli living. He thought she would be in some nice gated community living with the up-wardly mobile crowd, but that was far from the case. The Village was just as ghetto as the place he just left. The frown on his face as they drove through the gates spoke volumes.

"I'm working on my master's degree right now, and this is all I can afford, but the minute I'm able to move, I'll be on the first thing flying out of here."

Franky looked around at the run-down apartments; some of them looked like they were already condemned. He saw an old man marching like he was in the Russian army, and he was being followed by about five little kids who were marching just like him. He couldn't help but chuckle at the sight.

"That's General Mack," Kelli said, laughing. "He was in some war that left him a little loony upstairs, but he's harmless."

Kelli stopped at the mailbox and jumped out. Franky tried to soak in as much of his new environment as he could. Kelli got back in the car with a stack of letters and junk mail.

"How long have you been living here?" Franky asked.

"Well, this is where me and my mother moved to when we first left New Orleans. I think I was in the seventh grade. Then we moved back home and then back again, so overall, I would say about six or seven years. I've been in my own place for two years."

"Where is your mom now?"

"She's back in New Orleans. But I think you'll like living here. At least until we move. This place really isn't that bad. It looks worse than it really is, even though we do have some occasional inner-city activity. There are some nice kids out here. You have your bad ones, too," Kelli said, nodding toward a fat guy who was standing beside a BMW with chrome rims on it. There were a bunch of people standing around him as if he were the king chatting with his court.

"Who is that?" Franky asked.

"Some loser who calls himself Wicked. And from what I hear, he lives up to that moniker. It isn't hard to tell how he makes his money, but I guess he thinks that's cool."

Kelli parked in front of her apartment, and Franky got out of the car. He walked around to the trunk and got all of his belongings. The air-conditioned apartment was such a relief. Franky had forgotten how it felt to go into a house to escape the heat.

"You can put your things in that bedroom," Kelli said, pointing to the room across from hers. "I'll figure out someplace to put all of those bookshelves. That used to be

my office, so just ignore that stuff until I can find someplace for it."

Franky nodded and placed his suitcase on the floor by
the closet. He looked around and saw a full-size bed, a
nightstand, and a dresser. All of the furniture still had the
tags on them.

Kelli stood in the doorway watching Franky. He turned
around and gave her a look that said he would rather be
anywhere but here. He wanted to go back to New Orleans
with Nigel and Rico.

"It'll take some getting used to, but you'll be fine,
Franky. I know you've been through a lot, but you have a
bright future ahead of you."

"My dad said . . . ," Franky said before catching himself.
"Can I go outside and take a look around?"

"Sure," Kelli said, nodding. "But before you go, Franky,
I need to lay down some ground rules. I hate to put this
out there on your first day here, but we might as well get
started on the right track. You're going to have a curfew.
It's ten o'clock on school nights and twelve o'clock on the
weekends."

*Curfew? Nigel and Rico never asked me to come in the
house at a specific time,* he thought.

"You're also going to have to do chores around here.
The dishes and bathrooms are your responsibility. That
means they should always be clean. I don't like to see
dishes in the sink, so put them in the dishwasher. I will
not—let me repeat, I will not—have a dirty bathroom.
Don't pee on the toilet seat, and if you do, use some toilet
paper to clean it up. That's your bathroom, so make sure
it's spotless. I will clean mine, but yours is on you. I'm
waiting on your birth certificate to arrive from New Or-

leans, and once it does, you will be attending school. I expect homework done before you head outside. If you don't have any homework, then I'm going to need at least an hour of study time for myself. There is always something to study. And last but not least, no disrespect. Ever. I don't need to hear 'yes, ma'am' or 'no, ma'am,' but let's get along. I will do everything I'm supposed to do to make sure you have what you need, and all I ask in return is for you to follow those rules. *Comprende?*"

Franky nodded.

Kelli smiled and gave him another hug. "I missed you so much, Franky, and I'm glad you're here."

Once Kelli let him go, he walked out of the apartment.

This was the pits. He could already tell that this situation wasn't going to work out. He didn't like Kelli, and he knew that he needed to do something to get out of here. He walked around the complex until he found the basketball courts. When he walked up, there were about twenty kids on the blacktop playing. The game paused for a second as the players checked out the new guy. Once they chalked him up as harmless, they continued.

"What's up?" said a tall brown-skinned guy who was standing on the sideline watching the game. He extended his hand toward Franky. "Romeo."

"What's up, Romeo?" Franky said, shaking the boy's hand. "Franky."

"Do you ball?"

"Nah," Franky said. "I'm more of a football guy."

"Me too," Romeo said. "You live around here?"

"Just moved in a few minutes ago."

"That's what's up," Romeo said. "So you going to Tucker High?"

"I don't know where I'm going. Is that the school for this area?"

"Yep."

"I heard about Tucker. Y'all won the state championship a few times, right?"

"Yep."

"What position do you play?"

"Quarterback. Number one in the state, number three in the country. I wanna see those two guys who the pundits say are better than me," Romeo said, and Franky could tell this kid had a competitive spirit that would take him anywhere he wanted to go.

"Oh, yeah. I was gonna play at my last school, but then I had to move over here."

"Where did you go?"

"I was at M and M High," Franky said.

"Okay. M and M is straight. You know we can always use another good player," Romeo said. "What grade are you in?"

"Ninth."

"Oh, you're a youngster but still. We have a nice junior varsity program. You should come out."

The game on the court got rowdy, and two guys started to fight. Romeo shook his head and walked out onto the court and separated the combatants. He walked back and stood on the sideline like nothing had happened. One of the guys who was fighting walked over still jawing with the guy he got into it with.

"Yo, man," the short guy said. "Let's get out of here before I mess around and catch a case."

Romeo stood there with his arms folded, laughing.

"This is my man Amir," he said.

"What's good with ya, player? You live round here?" Amir said, balling his fist up and reaching out to Franky.

"Yeah. Franky," he said, and bumped his fist.

"I sure hate that you had to see me slap a fool on your first day here, but every now and then I gotta show these fools what the business is," Amir said. "He got pissed because I was shooting those jays in his face. Ain't my fault I got stupid game."

"I hear ya," Franky said, laughing because all he saw was Amir shooting air balls.

"Well, Franky," Romeo said. "We gotta roll. I hope to see you at school, man."

"His girl has him on a clock," Amir said. "If he misses a call, she whips that arse."

"Don't listen to this fool," Romeo said. "He's mad because he's still a virgin."

"How many times I gotta tell you I gets mine. Your interception waiting to happen," Amir said.

"Y'all take care," Franky said as they walked off arguing about something.

Franky decided that he was gonna force Kelli to send him back to New Orleans. He saw the guy who had been sitting on his BMW holding court when he first got to the apartments and walked over to him.

"What's up, whoadie?" Franky said, approaching cautiously. "Are you Wicked?"

"Depends on who's asking," said the fat guy with platinum teeth and a matching chain around his neck. Everything about his demeanor and clothes said "up to no good."

"I'm Franky," he said, thinking of a lie he could tell the

guy in order to get in good with him. "My cousin told me to come holla at you."

"Who yo cousin, youngster?" Wicked asked.

"Rico," Franky said. "I just moved out here, and he said you was cool and to tell you wassup."

"I don't know no Rico, but then again, I'm good with faces but bad with names. Ain't no telling," Wicked said, reaching out to shake Franky's hand. "What's up witcha?"

"Nuttin', man. I just moved out here and wanted to come say what's up and see if you had any work for me."

"So you looking for some work?"

"Yeah."

"Work-work or something to keep you busy?" Wicked asked.

"Just something to make a few dollars," Franky said. "I just got out of jail today. I'm not tryna go back."

"I hear ya. Well, I always need security. You wanna handle that?"

"That's cool," Franky said.

"Meet me tonight around midnight out here on the courts. I need to run and holla at this lil honey," Wicked said before getting in his car.

Franky watched him pull off and smiled. His plan was moving in the right direction. He was going to force his aunt to send him back to New Orleans.

28

Franky took a shower and stretched out across his bed. He was homesick again. He missed living with his cousins and thought he would give anything to be out of this soft and comfortable bed and back into the hard one he had had at the house with Nigel and Rico.

Kelli had come to his room and said good night twenty minutes ago, but she was still fiddling around the apartment. He wished she would hurry up and take her butt to bed so he could get on with his plan to get back to New Orleans. This was his third night living with her and still didn't like it. Kelli wasn't as bad as he thought she would be, but he wasn't interested in being that goody-two-shoes little boy she wanted him to be. Mr. Goody-two-shoes was dead. Being good in the hood was asking for trouble. People had to respect you, and he planned to get his right away in the Village. At least until he could get back with his own people.

He still missed Khadija and often wondered what she

was doing, how she was feeling, and if she was thinking about him.

Just yesterday, he took the MARTA bus out to her house while Kelli was at work with hopes of catching her outside, but to his surprise, the house was totally empty with a FOR SALE sign in the yard. He looked up at the window where he last saw her and realized that he would never see again.

Franky stood up and walked into the living room. He had been sneaking out every night since he had been there. His job with Wicked was putting one hundred dollars a night into his pocket, and the plan was to save up enough to get a plane ticket back to New Orleans. He peeked into Kelli's bedroom and found her fast asleep. He stepped away from her door and headed out to the basketball courts. The other guys who worked for Wicked weren't his type, so he kept to himself.

"What's good with ya?" Wicked said, motioning for one of his flunkies to give Franky a weapon.

Franky took his firearm and headed to his post. Just as he sat down, a guy walked up. He looked around the apartments like a tourist. Franky stood and went to meet him. It was his job to stop anyone from approaching Wicked. The fat man had many enemies, and he was paranoid.

"Hold up, man," Franky said to the guy who was casually strolling toward the basketball courts.

"Who are you talking to?" the guy said.

"I'm talking to you," Franky said, noticing the guy's bulging muscles. But they were no match for what he was holding in his hand.

The guy laughed at Franky and walked on as if he was a mere nuisance.

"Yo, man," Franky snapped as he hustled to get in front of the guy. "You deaf?"

The guy looked like he was about to rip Franky's head off but stopped when Wicked jumped up and called his name. They gave each other brotherly hugs, and Wicked picked the guy up and swung him around.

Franky backed off and went back to his post, but he wasn't going to let that guy's disrespect slide. He was tired of being that guy, and he wasn't about to start that here. Being Mr. Nice Guy was how he lost everything at his last place of residence.

Franky sat back and watched the guy and Wicked act like long-lost buddies. He didn't like either one of them but especially the guy who blew him off.

After about a fifteen-minute chat session, Wicked jumped into his car and drove off. The guy remained on the courts looking around. Then he sat down, leaned back on the bench, and seemed to be having a peaceful night. Franky pointed his gun up in the air and squeezed the trigger. There was a loud boom, and out of nowhere he was hit and forced to the ground. That old stink man who was marching the kids around was lying on top of him. He tried to get up, but the old bum was too strong.

The guy on the bench walked over and stood over the two of them.

"Are you shooting at me?" he said. "Let him up, General Mack."

The old man stood up, and Franky jumped to his feet. General Mack held his arm so he couldn't go anywhere.

"I asked you a question," the guy said calmly.

General Mack hauled off and slapped Franky on the back of the head. "He's talking to you, dummy."

"Man," Franky said. "If you put your nasty, crusty hands on me again, I will—"

"Franky!" Kelli screamed. "What in the world are you doing out here?"

Franky looked at his aunt and wanted to run, but instead he just dropped his head in defeat. Nothing was working out for him.

"I'm sick of you already, boy. I hear gunshots—then I look in your room and you're gone. Tell me that wasn't you out here shooting."

"That was him," General Mack said. "Sure as a dog got a tail. It was him."

"Kelli," the guy who had dissed Franky said.

"Kwame?"

"Yeah. How are ya?"

"I was doing okay until my nephew decided he was going to sneak out and try his best to go back to jail," she said, reaching out and slapping Franky hard across the face.

"I shot up in the air," he said in protest.

"Where did you get a gun?"

Franky looked away, holding his face.

General Mack picked up the gun and marched away in his communist trot.

"Get your lil narrow butt in that apartment," Kelli said.

Franky walked back to the apartment. His plan had unraveled, because now she was really going to keep a close eye on him. He was stuck. He walked inside and sat on his bed. Five minutes later, Kelli walked in, and made a beeline for his room.

"You listen to me and you listen good. Your birth certificate came in the mail today. You will start school tomorrow, and you better get your act together. You will not be
a bum, Franky. It's just not going to happen," she said,
shaking her head. "This little superthug act—the tattoos
and outlaw attitude—is not you. You weren't raised like
that, and I'm not going to let you become that.

"Now, I don't know what Nigel and Rico have been
teaching you over there, but it's not going to fly here. You
will be somebody. So here's my proposal. You will either
do what you're supposed to do and live a peaceful life, or
do what you're supposed to do and I make it hard. But either way you will do what you're supposed to do. Your father asked me to take care of you, and that's what I'm
gonna do, but it's up to you how you want it."

Franky sighed. This thug life was for the birds. His gangster days were over. He took off his clothes and got in bed.

29

Jimrose Christian Academy was one of the largest private schools in the state of Georgia. Kelli drove Franky through the gates, and they were met by an old white man who stopped cars that didn't have a sticker on the windshield.

"Here for registration," Kelli said.

"Name," he said with a pleasant smile.

"Bourgeois," she said.

"Building six," the guard said. "He's all set. His welcome package and schedule will be waiting for him on the second floor. There will always be a parking sticker in there for you, ma'am."

"Thank you," Kelli said, and pulled into one of the most prestigious schools in the country.

Franky looked around and took in the campus. This place was huge. He saw the football field and smiled. The school reminded him of the one he had attended back in Jefferson Parish. They arrived between classes, and hundreds of kids were going about their business. The school was mostly white kids, but he saw his share of blacks and Hispanics, too.

JCA taught kids between the ages of four and eighteen years. Franky couldn't help but feel like he had died and gone to heaven. He looked at Kelli and for the first time in a long time smiled.

"What are you smiling about? I didn't even know you could smile," she said, smiling herself.

"Please tell me this is my school."

"Yep," she said. "This is your school."

Franky couldn't believe his luck. He reached over and gave his auntie a big hug. "I'm sorry, Aunt Kelli. I didn't mean to act so stupid. It just seems things have been going from bad to worse since my mother died."

"I understand, but your father is with you. Trust me—sometimes I feel like he's right in the room talking to me."

"Yeah," Franky said. "Me too."

"It's the weirdest thing because he seems so real," Kelli said as they walked into a large building and over to the elevators. They got on one and went up a floor.

"Why didn't I come here when I first moved here?" Franky said. "I've always liked school."

"School is a good thing," Kelli said. "This place costs fifteen thousand dollars a year. They don't let any riffraff in here, so make me proud."

"Well, my riffraff days are done," Franky said.

They walked into a room, and Kelli picked up an envelope and signed her name.

"You're all set," she said, handing him the envelope. "This is your schedule. I'll be here to pick you up at four. Meet me outside."

Franky reached out and hugged his aunt again.

"Okay," Kelli said before walking away. "Make me proud."

"I will," Franky said as he watched her leave. He stayed on the second-floor looking down at the sea of red polo shirts and khaki pants. The kids were changing classes, and his eyes found a little brown-skinned boy who looked to be around six or seven years old. The little boy reminded Franky of himself when he was his age, and he couldn't help but smile at the memory. Just as he was taking his walk down memory lane, his thoughts were interrupted by two white guys.

"Who are you?" a freckled-face boy with orange hair asked.

"Who's asking?" Franky shot back.

"What's with the tattoo? Are you like some kind of thug?" the other boy said.

"Nope," Franky said, sensing that these guys weren't a part of the Jimrose Christian Academy's welcoming committee.

"Well," Freckles said, leaning in close to Franky's face, "we have a good school here and we don't want any of your kind coming in here messing it up."

"What's my kind?" Franky asked with a smirk.

Freckles looked him up and down, then turned away and spat on the walkway.

"Before you know it, we'll have people riding around here with old cars painted the color of a Snickers bar with big rims on it. They have schools for your kind. Why don't you go back to the hood?" the other boy added.

"Yeah," Freckles said as he poked Franky in his chest. "So if you think for one second you're going to come around here with that ghetto crap, you have another think coming. *Comprende?*"

"If you ever touch me again, I will break my foot off in your . . ." Franky started to say, but was cut off when somebody grabbed his hand. He snatched it away and looked at the culprit. His eyes grew wide, then he had to do a double take. All of a sudden, the two clowns were no longer of any interest to him.

"Khadija," he said, as he had to make sure it was really her. She had cut her hair short like Rihanna and wore two small diamond earrings in her ears instead of the big loops that she used to wear when she was at M&M High.

"Franky," she said with a blank look on her face. "What are you doing here?"

"This is my school now. Today is my first day. I moved in with my aunt."

"Remember what we said, *homeboy*," Freckles said as he and his friend walked away.

"Trouble seems to find you, huh?" Khadija said.

"I guess so. They came up calling me a thug, but I'm not concerned with those idiots," Franky said, smiling from ear to ear.

Khadija noticed his tattoo. "Why did you do that to your arm?"

Franky pulled his sleeve up above his shoulder and exposed a big red heart with her name in the center of it.

Khadija opened her mouth to speak, but no words came out. She placed a hand over her chest and stared into his eyes.

"I did that because I never wanted to be without you," he said. "I thought I'd never see you again. But last night, I said a prayer and I asked God not to take you out of my life. And here you are."

Khadija stepped closer to him and slid her arms around

his waist. Franky hugged her to him, and they embraced for a long time.

"We are going to be late for class," he said, finally pulling away. "Are you trying to get me in trouble on my first day of school?"

Khadija had tears in her eyes when she looked up at Franky. "I missed you, shawty."

Franky smiled and couldn't think of a sweeter name to be called.

"I missed you, too. Now let's get to class."

AT THE CROSSROADS

Travis Hunter

ABOUT THIS GUIDE

The following questions are intended to
enhance your group's reading of
AT THE CROSSROADS.

DISCUSSION QUESTIONS

1. Franky was a fish out of water living in the ghetto. Do you think living in the hood makes you bad?

2. Franky and his cousins had the best clothes but didn't put any value on education. Why do you think that was the case for them?

3. Franky's relationship with Khadija brought him a great deal of joy, but after one incident, her parents shut that down. Were they already suspicious of him?

4. Rico called down to the swamps to help his cousin out. Do you believe in voodoo?

5. Nigel seemed to be a really good guy. Do you think his life would've been different if he had had some real guidance?

6. Why do you think being ghetto is a badge of honor for some in the black community?

7. Once Franky was in a different situation and realized that he was going to be held accountable, he changed. Do teens crave discipline?

8. Why do you think Franky wanted to go back with his cousin so bad?

PROLOGUE
ROMEO

I paced the rooftop of my apartment complex with a .40-caliber Glock pistol in the palm of my hand, sweat pouring off of my closely cropped head. Fear had a stranglehold on me, and my heart threatened to beat its way out of my chest. I struggled to control my breathing as I eased over to the edge of the building and took in the sight of the only place I had ever called home. That's when I realized that life as I knew it was over.

A nervous chuckle escaped my lips. How dare I ever allow myself to dream of a life outside of this box I was placed in since the day I was born? First my brother's dreams were snatched away, then mine. The more I thought about it, the more I realized my life was doomed from the start.

1

ROMEO

"You ever cheated on Ngiai?" my best friend, Amir, asked me as we walked home from school on a wooded path toward our home in the busted-in and burned-out subsidized projects. Atlanta's Village Apartments had been my home for the last ten years of my life, and although it was a pretty rough spot, I liked it.

"Who is that?" I smiled.

"Whatever. You a player but you ain't stupid."

"I don't cheat. I'm a good boy," I said.

"Man," Amir said, shaking his head. "How you function with all those girls up in your face all the time?"

"The same way you function with none in your face. I just keep it moving."

"What? You crazy. I got more than my share of the honeys, player. I just keep my business to myself," Amir said.

"Yeah, that's not all you keep to yourself. But you should embrace your virginity and stop being ashamed of it."

"You crazy. I lost my virginity a long time ago, lil buddy," Amir bragged his lie.

"Yeah, but Fancy and her four sisters don't count," I said, wiggling my fingers in his face.

"Whatever, homie," he said, smacking my hand down. "Like I said, I keep mine's to myself. I'm respectful of the woman I spend my private time with. Don't need to run around here telling you low-self-esteem-having clowns 'bout my business."

"Yeah, okay," I said.

"What the . . . ," Amir said, stopping in his tracks as we noticed the path to our apartments was cut off by a six-foot-high wrought-iron fence.

"I guess we're moving on up, Amir," I said, running my fingers along the black iron. "I always wanted to live in a gated community."

Amir folded his arms. His face wore a disgusted scowl. He was quiet and his breathing was measured. He seemed to be analyzing the situation we had before us. One of the men working on the gate nodded at me and I nodded back.

"Don't be speaking to no Mexicans, Romeo," Amir snapped. He huffed a frustrated breath, then found his stride along the fence line. "Those people are the worst of the worst. The white man tells them to put up a fence locking black folks in and they jump on the job. No standards. Anything for a buck," Amir said. "You don't see what's going on?"

Amir kept me laughing. He was a walking worrywart who believed the government was secretly conspiring to eliminate the black man from the face of the earth. Maybe that was the reason his hair was turning gray at the tender

age of seventeen. He claimed his dad was a political prisoner, but in reality he was just a prisoner who got caught
selling drugs.

"Nah, why don't you tell me what's going on, Reverend
Al Sharpton Jr.?" I said.

"This is nothing more than the government's way of
preparing us for incarceration. My daddy sent me a book,
and he said the only reason they call where we live the
'projects' is because the powers that be are doing a project on how to eliminate our black butts."

"Your daddy's a genius, dude. You are so lucky that he
imparts such deep wisdom on the world," I said sarcastically. "That's why they keep him locked up, man. He's too
smart to unleash on the world."

"Okay, see, you think this is a game. You're one of those
dum-dums who can't call a spade a spade. I can't believe
you can't see what's going on, Romeo. They tryna condi-
tion us to being surrounded by fences. And what does a
prison have? A bunch of doggone gates." He looked at me
like I was the dumbest person ever to take a breath.
"That's what's wrong with black people. We don't think."

"So now you got a problem with black people too?"

His eyes almost popped out of his head. "My *biggest*
problem is with black people. We the worst of the worst."

"I thought you just said Mexicans were the worst of the
worst."

"Hell . . . neither one of us are worth a red cent. But I'll
tell you what—black people are the only group of people
on this earth who just don't care how we look on TV. We're
just happy to be on TV. Master want me to play a pimp and
degrade my sisters . . . Okay." He mocked a wide-eyed min-
strel character. "They be like, 'You ain't even gotta pay me

that much—just put me on TV so people can think I'm somebody and I'll beat that ho to death.'"

I laughed as I always did when Amir went off on one of his race tangents.

"Now, I will say one thing about Mexicans," he said. "They will work."

"Black people work too," I defended. "This country was built on the backs of black people."

"Man, that was three hundred years ago. And we ain't done jack since. I guess we're resting."

"What about Barack Obama?"

"Man, whatever. One man out of two million and you want me to jump up and clap."

"Shut up, Amir," I said.

"I'm just saying," Amir said, sticking his middle finger up at a big poster of a fancy-dressed real estate mogul whose face was plastered on the side of a MARTA bus station. "We done lost all of our pride, man. There's nothing sacred in the black community anymore."

"Why do you stick your finger up at that picture every day?" I asked.

"Do you know who that is?"

"Nope," I said.

"Damn, Rome. You gotta get a little more involved in something other than rap videos and SportsCenter. That's the fool who owns all of these apartment complexes around here. Mr. Slumlord himself. He's riding around in Bentleys and we living in the hood. I don't have a problem with him getting paid, but I do have a problem if he's getting paid from keeping us poor."

"Now, in all of your extensive research, how did you find out that keeping us in the hood makes him rich?"

Amir shook his head again. "It's a good thing you can throw a football, because you 'bout one stupid little boy."

"Enlighten me, Dr. Know-It-All."

Amir shook his head. "Lord, I swear my people are going to perish due to stupidity. The government pays big money to people who take on section eight and subsidize housing. Damn Democrats."

"So you are a Republican, Amir?"

"Not really, I'm Amir. The government is full of crap."

"Shut up, Amir."

"That man on that poster is no different than those slave catchers who used to chase down other blacks for the plantation owner."

"You can find a way to compare everything to slavery," I said, growing tired of Amir's Black Panther moment.

"Okay, name one thing that we as black folks can't find a joke about."

I searched my brain but couldn't come up with anything.

"I'm telling you, Rome. You can think about it until your black face turns blue, but you ain't coming up with nothing. We laugh about everything, a hee hee hee. Even slavery. I bet you won't find a Jewish person laughing about the Holocaust."

"How you gonna judge an entire race based on a few clowns?" I said, getting pulled back in again.

My boy Amir was a character, and I loved getting him riled up. All five-foot-two inches of him. He had a caramel-brown complexion and a big gray patch of hair in the middle of his head. He gave me that Boo Boo the Fool look again.

"We allow those clowns to prosper. We celebrate these

fools and make 'em spokespeople for the black community. Have you ever seen the Ying Yang Twins? What about Gucci Mane?"

I had to laugh at that one.

"And that's who we have representing us. I rest my case," he said, throwing his hands up in the air.

"You know, Amir, you should've been born in the fifties or sixties so you could really have something to complain about."

"Oh, you think it's all gravy now, Mr. Dumb Football Player? Racism worse now than it was in the sixties, only now they don't wear white sheets—they wear suits. That's because they're the CEOs of the record labels and television stations. That includes the black CEOs too. If they really gave a hoot about helping blacks, then they wouldn't go and find the most ignorantiest people they can find and put them on TV for little kids to look up to. I swear, I wish I could go on a Nat Turner spree and get away with it."

"*Ignorantiest?* That's not even a word. And you got the nerve to call me dumb."

"It's these public schools, man," Amir said, shaking his head. "But you know what I mean."

Our low-level political debate came to a halt when we saw a few of the project natives standing around a fancy car belonging to a neighborhood hustler name Pete "Wicked" Sams.

Wicked had a few of the locals' undivided attention as he told tall tales of his life as an outlaw. He stopped midsentence when he saw me.

"Romey Rome," Wicked called, waving his arm for me to come over and join him. "Holla at me."

"What's up, Wicked?" I said, throwing my hand up in the air and not missing a stride. I knew better. Wicked would have me out there with him all day long talking about what he used to do on the football field. The more he told the story, the better a player he became, and I had heard it so much that by now, to hear him tell it, he was better than every player in the NFL.

"Come here, boy," Wicked called out, which was more like a command.

"I'm in a hurry, man," I said, slowing a little.

"You in too much of a hurry that you can't come and holla at your boy?" Wicked said, playing the guilt card.

Amir shot me a look and shook his head.

"Man, let me go and holla at this fool for a minute," I said, finally relenting.

"You go right ahead. I ain't about to sit up here all day listening to some fool who calls himself Wicked," Amir said. "I'm going home to handle some business."

"A'ight, man. I'll see you later," I said.

"Rock on, black man," Amir said, throwing up his peace sign as he hurried to his building.

"Where the militant midget running off to?" Wicked asked me as I walked over to him and gave him a fraternity-brother-like hug.

"Home, I guess," I said, shaking a few more hands.

"So are you sitting on the bench, or you getting in the game?"

"Don't even try me like that," I said. "How's life treating you, Pete?"

"Beating me down, but hey," Wicked said, rubbing his ample stomach. "I'm eating good."

"I see," I said, eyeing the Buddha-like thing hanging on the front of his body. "You look like you're about six months pregnant."

A few of the flunkies laughed but quickly zipped their lips when Wicked jerked his head in their direction.

"What you do last game?" Wicked asked, turning back to me.

"Threw for two hundred and ran for a hundred but we lost, so it didn't matter."

"Damn, boy, you the high school all world, ain't cha?"

"Nah, just doing me," I said.

"Keep doing what you doing. I be hearing about cha. You got a lil buzz going round. You know I blew my career up hanging out here in these damn streets. I'm telling you, Rome, I used to be a beast." Wicked's eyes widened with excitement.

Here we go, I thought to myself.

"Ray Lewis ain't had nothing on me, boy. I used to break bones. Crack! I'm talking about giving coaches straight up sleepless nights tryna figure out how to block me. Had lil quarterbacks like you in straight panics. Rome, I would've broke you up, boy."

"You too slow, Wicked," I said, shaking my head. "You wouldn't stand a chance."

"You crazy. Ask your brother 'bout me, boy. Matter of fact, come by the crib. I got tapes to prove my word ain't a lie."

"Whatever. I don't wanna see any tapes. If you were all that, then why ain't you in the league?"

"See, my problem was I wanted that fast money." Wicked spread his arms and nodded toward his black 745 BMW.

"Ain't doing too bad but if I could do it all again, I might've paid for this ride with different dollars."

"It's not too late," I said.

"Look at you. Mr. Opportunistic. Always looking on the bright side."

"You mean *optimistic.*"

"That's what I said."

"No, you said *opportunistic.*"

Wicked turned to one of his flunkies. "What did I say?"

"You said it right," said Mark, a tall skinny kid whose only job on earth was to be Wicked's yes-man.

"Whatever," I said. "How are you gonna ask somebody who failed pre-K to answer a question about a word with more than one syllable?"

"Who you talking to?" Mark said, puffing out his little birdlike chest and yanking the chain of his vicious-looking pit bull.

"You," I said, not in the least bit concerned with him or his dog.

"Mark, shut yo mouth, boy. We can't have Romeo out here hurting up his hands on the likes of you," Wicked said, pushing his flunky away.

"I ain't worried about his hands. I'ma let this damn dog go on him."

"I'm petrified," I said. "Oh, my bad. That's three syllables. I meant to say, I'm scared."

"Come on, Rome." Wicked went into his boxer's stance. "I'm tired of you and all *your* mouth."

I still didn't move. Pete was my older brother Kwame's friend, so he looked at me as if I was his little brother. That was the only reason I could get away with talking to him the way I did. Anyone else would be picking up a few teeth right about now.

"Boy, how old is you now?" Wicked asked.

"Seventeen."

"And you what?" Wicked stood in front of me and placed his hand at his head to measure who was the tallest. "Six feet."

"Six-one," I said, standing up. "You know my brother might be coming home in a few days. His parole hearing's tomorrow."

"Aw, man." Wicked swatted away my concern with his chubby hand. "That lil crack charge ain't 'bout nuttin'. Ain't no *might* about it—he coming home. And you tell him I said come holla at me the minute he touches town."

"I can't wait for him to get out of that place. He's been gone too long," I said, thinking about how much I missed the guy who was far more than a big brother to me. He was also the only father figure I'd ever had. Everything I knew, I learned it from Kwame.

"Two years." Wicked frowned up his face. "Man, that ain't jack. I can do that without a snack."

"Two years is a long time."

"For you maybe, but not for my dog. See you . . . Big Nana sheltered you too much. Wouldn't let you cuss, made you do your homework, and had you up in piano lessons like you was gonna be a black Rocketeer or some-body," Wicked said, drawing laughter from his cronies.

"There you go. I'm outta here," I said, reaching out to tap his fist with mine.

"A'ight. Tell Kwame I said come holla at a player when he gets himself settled," Wicked said, touching his heart.

"Okay," I said, walking away and frowning at the ludicrous thought of my brother putting himself back into the same situation that got him arrested in the first place. I wasn't sure what led to his arrest, because everyone kept the details from me, but I was almost one hundred percent sure Wicked had something to do with it.

"Rome." Wicked stood and shuffled his three-hundred-pound frame over to me. "Hold up, boy. You always rushing off somewhere." He placed a roll of money in my palm.

"What's this for?"

"Just a lil something something. Make sure Kwame knows I gave you that. If . . . When he gets home, give him some of it and tell him I said we need to talk."

I nodded and we shared another brotherly hug.

Living in the Village Apartments, aka "The V," gave you an edge, a hardness that was essential if you were going to survive the everyday rigors of life in subsidized housing. But it was also a trap waiting to close its jaws around you at the slightest slipup. I made my way through the breezeways between the buildings and stopped when I saw General Mack, our neighborhood nutcase and shell-shocked war veteran, marching a line of five-year-olds as if they were in basic training.

"Hut two, three, four. Pick ya legs up, soldier. Hey, pay attention, boy. You gonna mess around and get yourself shot," he sang with all seriousness.

"Good Lord. That man is nuttier than a fruitcake," I said, shaking my head at the spectacle before me. The kids seemed to be having fun, so all I could do was laugh before heading upstairs to the apartment I shared with my nana.

HAVEN'T HAD ENOUGH? CHECK OUT THESE GREAT SERIES FROM DAFINA BOOKS!

DRAMA HIGH

by L. Divine

Follow the adventures of a young sistah who's learning that life in the hood is nothing compared to life in high school.

THE FIGHT	SECOND CHANCE	JAYD'S LEGACY
ISBN: 0-7582-1633-5	ISBN: 0-7582-1635-1	ISBN: 0-7582-1637-8
FRENEMIES	LADY J	COURTIN' JAYD
ISBN: 0-7582-2532-6	ISBN: 0-7582-2534-2	ISBN: 0-7582-2536-9
HUSTLIN'	KEEP IT MOVIN'	HOLIDAZE
ISBN: 0-7582-3105-9	ISBN: 0-7582-3107-5	ISBN: 0-7582-3109-1
CULTURE CLASH	COLD AS ICE	PUSHIN'
ISBN: 0-7582-3111-3	ISBN: 0-7582-3113-X	ISBN: 0-7582-3115-6

BOY SHOPPING

by Nia Stephens

An exciting "you pick the ending" series that lets the reader pick Mr. Right.

BOY SHOPPING	LIKE THIS AND LIKE THAT	GET MORE
ISBN: 0-7582-1929-6	ISBN: 0-7582-1931-8	ISBN:0-7582-1933-4

DEL RIO BAY

by Paula Chase

A wickedly funny series that explores friendship, betrayal, and how far some people will go for popularity.

SO NOT THE DRAMA	DON'T GET IT TWISTED	THAT'S WHAT'S UP!
ISBN: 0-7582-1859-1	ISBN: 0-7582-1861-3	ISBN: 0-7582-2582-2
	WHO YOU WIT?	FLIPPING THE SCRIPT
	ISBN: 0-7582-2584-9	ISBN: 0-7582-2586-5

PERRY SKKY JR.

by Stephanie Perry Moore

An inspirational series that follows the adventures of a high school football star as he balances faith and the temptations of teen life.

PRIME CHOICE	PRESSING HARD	PROBLEM SOLVED
ISBN: 0-7582-1863-X	ISBN: 0-7582-1872-9	ISBN: 0-7582-1874-5
	PRAYED UP	PROMISE KEPT
	ISBN: 0-7582-2538-5	ISBN: 0-7582-2540-7